Mortals

Of

Kandahar II

"The Beginning"

- Garima Yadav

The Beginning

Acknowledgements

Writing this novel has been a journey of passion, introspection, and discovery, and it would not have been possible without the unwavering support of the incredible people in my life.

First and foremost, I am deeply grateful to my family—my husband, whose love, patience, and encouragement gave me the strength to bring this story to life.

To my parents.

A special thanks to my daughter, whose curiosity and joy remind me of the beauty of storytelling.

This novel owes its foundation to the timeless inspirations of history, culture, and human resilience. To the readers of my previous works, including Musings of Enkindled Heart and Mortals of Kandahar your love for my words fuels my creative spirit.

Finally, to you, my readers, thank you for allowing me to share this world with you. Your time, imagination, and trust mean more than words can express.

Synopsis

Mortals of Kandahar II "*The Beginning*" is an epic continuation of the journey first unraveled in Mortals of Kandahar. The novel begins with a fractured Kandahar, reeling from the fallout of power struggles, betrayal and chaos.

As ancient forces stir, Arian, bound by his family legacy as the grandson of Rajvanta, uncovers secrets buried in time. Meanwhile, Aryanath, Darius, and Kyra-now seasoned figures in their 40s—return with wisdom and scars from past battles.

In "*The Beginning*", bonds are tested, loyalty is questioned, and the thin line between survival and destruction blurs. The novel explores themes of leadership, trust, and the cost of ambition.

This gripping sequel sets the tone for an expansive saga, unraveling the mysteries of the past and laying the foundation for a future. "*The Beginning*" is not just about rebuilding but about discovering who you are when faced with the insurmountable.

"Mortals of Kandahar" is a delightfully alluring tale of love, destiny, and the yearning for fulfillment amidst the intricate dance of aspirations and ambition.

"Mortals of Kandahar" is a lyrical exploration of human's soul - What price do we pay for the path we choose. This novel is a journey through the shadows and light of desire, a tale that lingers long after the final page is turned.

Table of Contents

From

Shadows of the Past

Chapter 1 – The Echoes of Kandahar

There was a gentle breeze, carrying with it the faint fragrance of freshly watered roses from the palace gardens. The city awoke like a masterpiece unveiled, bathed in golden light that danced across its ancient walls and winding streets. Merchants opened their stalls, the melody of their morning calls blending with the distant hum of temple bells. From her chambers high above, Vajra watched her city come alive, a perfect harmony of beauty and resilience.

Though nineteen years had passed since her birth, the weight of her lineage pressed heavily upon her shoulders. Kandahar was more than just her home; it was her inheritance, her responsibility, and, perhaps, her greatest test. It had endured wars, witnessed betrayals, and celebrated fleeting moments of peace under her parents, Kyra and Darius, now in their forties. But Vajra knew peace was fragile. It whispered of promise while shadows lingered at the edges, waiting for their moment to strike.

The room behind her was silent, save for the faint rustling of parchment. Her childhood friend and closest confidant, Arian, sat cross-legged on the floor, poring over reports. Arian had been raised in the palace, his heritage rooted in the royal bloodlines of Kandahar. As the grandson of Rajvanta—a once-powerful ruler whose reign ended in tragedy—he had been brought into Darius's court to ensure his safety and preserve the lineage of his family.

Darius and Kyra had treated Arian like a son, and over the years, he had earned his place not just as Vajra's friend, but as her advisor. Though his ancestry carried a shadow of past betrayal, his loyalty to the royal family was unquestionable. His sharp wit and pragmatic mind often balanced Vajra's fiery spirit, making him an invaluable presence by her side.

~

"You're awake early," Arian remarked without looking up, his voice carrying the faintest hint of amusement. "That's never a good sign."
Vajra turned from the window, a small smile playing at her lips. "The city speaks to me in the quiet hours.
Before the noise begins, I can feel its heartbeat."
Arian chuckled, setting aside the scrolls. "Kandahar's heartbeat or your restless thoughts? Tell me, Princess, what keeps you awake? A dream of adventure or the shadow of something darker?"

She hesitated, her smile fading. "Both, perhaps."

 Before she could elaborate, the heavy door to her chambers creaked open, and General Ashwavarna, the commander of Kandahar's armies, stepped inside. His armour glinted in the morning light, and the scar cutting across his weathered face told stories of battles hard-fought and narrowly won.

"Apologies for the intrusion, Princess," Ashwavarna said, bowing briefly. "But there's something you need to see."
Vajra's heart quickened. "What is it?"

Ashwavarna glanced at Arian, then back to Vajra. "A rider arrived before dawn, bearing a message from the northern frontier. The villages there have been abandoned. Every man, woman, and child-gone."

Arian shot to his feet. "Gone? How? Fled or taken?"
"Neither," Ashwavarna said grimly. "There are no signs of struggle, no tracks leading away. It's as if they vanished into thin air."

Vajra frowned, her mind racing. "And the message?"
Ashwavarna held out a sealed scroll. Vajra broke the wax and unrolled the parchment, her eyes scanning the hurried script. The words chilled her:

Beware the shadows that whisper. The winds carry more than rumours.

Arian stepped closer, peering over her shoulder.
"What does it mean?"

"I don't know," Vajra admitted, though unease stirred in her chest. "But we must find out. Dispatch scouts to the north immediately, and double the guard at the city gates. I won't take any chances."

Ashwavarna nodded and turned to leave. "It will be done."

As the door closed behind him, Arian spoke, his voice low. "You feel it too, don't you? The weight of something... coming."

 Vajra didn't respond immediately. Her gaze drifted back to the temple in the distance, its stones gleaming like silent sentinels.

"Yes," she finally said. "Kandahar has known peace for too long. The echoes of the past always return, Arian. And this time, I fear they will demand more from us than ever before."

And as the first rays of sunlight illuminated the city, Vajra knew one thing for certain: the shadows were stirring, and Kandahar's peace would soon shatter.

Chapter 2 — The Whispering Winds

The winds that swept through Kandahar that evening carried with them an unsettling chill, rustling the banners atop the city walls and whispering through the stone corridors of the palace.

They seemed almost alive, slipping into cracks and crevices, carrying secrets from lands far beyond the horizon.

Vajra stood on the eastern balcony of the palace, her sharp gaze fixed on the darkening skies. The day's warmth had faded into an uneasy twilight, and the stillness in the air felt unnatural. Below her, the city bustled as usual, unaware of the strange energy creeping through the night.

"It's unlike you to linger here after sunset," Arian remarked as he approached, his footsteps soft against the stone floor.

Vajra turned, offering him a faint smile. "The winds feel different tonight. As if they're trying to speak."

Arian gave a light laugh, though his expression betrayed concern. "You've been spending too much time with the temple priests. Next, you'll tell me you've heard the gods themselves whispering in the breeze."

Vajra crossed her arms, leaning against the balcony rail. "You don't feel it, Arian? The unease? The sense that something is coming?"

He sighed, stepping beside her. "I feel it. But it's no use dwelling on things we can't see or name. Until we have answers, we must prepare for all possibilities."

Before Vajra could respond, a shadowy figure emerged from the corridor behind them. General Ashwavarna's commanding presence filled the space as he bowed slightly, his armour glinting under the torchlight.

"Princess. Arian," Ashwavarna greeted them, his voice low but urgent. "The scouts sent to the northern frontier have returned."

Vajra straightened. "What have they found?"
Ashwavarna's grim expression deepened.
"They found nothing, Princess. Not a single
survivor. The villages remain eerily intact-no
signs of struggle, no tracks, no bodies. Just...
emptiness."

Arian frowned. "No bodies? Not even the
livestock?"
Ashwavarna shook his head. "Not even the
livestock.

It's as if the entire region was swallowed by
the earth."
Vajra's brow furrowed, her mind racing. "And
the winds? Did they carry any signs-smoke,
scents, anything unusual?"

"The winds carry only silence, Princess,"
Ashwavarna replied. "And that is what
troubles me most."

Vajra turned back to the horizon, her grip
tightening on the balcony's stone rail. "Silence
in a place where life once thrived... it feels
unnatural."

Ashwavarna hesitated before speaking again.
"There is one more thing. The scouts spoke
of strange markings etched into the ground

near one of the villages. Symbols none of
them recognise."

"Symbols?" Arian asked, his tone sharpening.
"Did they draw them?"
"They tried," Ashwavarna said, producing a
piece of parchment from his satchel. He
handed it to Vajra.
She unrolled it, her eyes narrowing at the
crude drawing. The symbol was intricate yet
unnervingly chaotic, a spiral-like pattern
surrounded by jagged lines and strange runes.
Something about it sent a shiver down her
spine.

"I've seen this before," Arian murmured, his
voice distant.

Vajra turned to him. "Where?"

Arian hesitated. "In the old archives, among
Rajvanta's writings. My grandfather spoke of a
similar symbol... linked to an ancient sect. A
forgotten faction that once sought to tear
Kandahar apart."

Ashwavarna's jaw tightened. "If they've
returned, we must act swiftly. We cannot
allow these whispers of old enemies to grow
into roars."

Vajra nodded, her voice steady despite the unease in her chest. "We need more information. Send word to the temple priests. If these symbols are tied to the past, they may know their meaning."

"And what of the council?" Arian asked.
"We'll tell them," Vajra replied. "But not yet. I don't want panic to spread before we know what we're dealing with."

The winds picked up again, tugging at her hair as if to echo her thoughts. As the three of them stood in silence, staring out into the dark, Vajra felt a deep resolve settle within her.

Whatever the winds carried—be it whispers of the past or warnings of the future-she would face it. For Kandahar. For her people.

Chapter 3 - The Warrior's Quest

The symbol etched into the parchment lingered in Vajra's thoughts, even as she descended into the depths of the palace archives later that night. The air grew colder as she and Arian made their way through the narrow stone corridors, the flickering torchlight casting eerie shadows on the ancient walls.
Behind them, Kyra, Darius, Aryanath, and General Ashwavarna followed in silence.

"This place hasn't changed," Kyra murmured, her voice soft but laced with unease. "It still feels as though the walls are watching."

Vajra glanced back at her mother, sensing the tension in her voice. Kyra rarely spoke of her time in the hidden chambers beneath the palace, where years ago, she and Aryanath had uncovered secrets of Kandahar's forgotten past. Whatever they had found had been carefully hidden again-sealed away to protect the city from forces best left undisturbed.

They stopped before an imposing iron door, its surface engraved with faded inscriptions in a script so ancient even the scholars of Kandahar struggled to decipher it.

"This is where we left the relics," Aryanath said, stepping forward. The years had tempered his once-youthful fire, but his eyes still burned with the wisdom and courage of a warrior. "What lies beyond this door may hold the answers we seek-or awaken dangers we cannot control."

"Then we have no choice but to proceed," Vajra said firmly, her gaze unwavering. "If these symbols are tied to Kandahar's past, we must uncover their meaning before it's too late."

Darius stepped forward, placing a reassuring hand on his daughter's shoulder. "Together, we will face whatever lies ahead."

With a nod from Darius, General Ashwavarna and Arian pushed open the heavy door. It groaned in protest, revealing a chamber cloaked in darkness.

Vajra stepped inside, holding the torch high, and her breath caught as the light illuminated the relics.

The chamber was a treasure trove of Kandahar's history. Ancient scrolls, faded maps, and forgotten weapons lay carefully arranged alongside jewelled artefacts and carved tablets. In the centre of the room, resting on a pedestal, was the most revered relic of all—a golden disc inscribed with cryptic markings.

Kyra approached the disc, her fingers grazing its surface as if reacquainting herself with an old memory. "This disc was once the key to unraveling the mystery of Alexander's edicts," she said, her voice reverent. "It is said to hold the wisdom of warriors and scholars who came before us. But we never uncovered all its secrets."

Vajra turned to her mother. "And these edicts - could they be connected to the symbols found in the northern frontier?"

"It's possible," Aryanath interjected, picking up one of the scrolls. "The symbols you described bear a resemblance to the markings we found on this disc years ago. They may be part of a forgotten language or code-something deliberately hidden from history."

As they examined the relics, Arian unrolled a brittle map, its edges frayed with time. "Look here," he said, pointing to a faint outline. "This marking near the northern frontier... it matches the symbol we saw on the parchment. It's not just a place. It's a waypoint—a marker for something buried or hidden."

"A trail," General Ashwavarna concluded. "If these symbols are part of a larger message, then this map may lead us to its origin."

Kyra exchanged a troubled glance with Darius. "We sealed this chamber because we feared what its secrets might unleash. If the symbols are resurfacing, it means someone-or something-has unearthed a piece of this past."

"And they may already be ahead of us," Arian added, his voice grim. "The silence in those villages could be their doing. They may be trying to finish what they started centuries ago."

Vajra's jaw tightened. "Then we cannot waste time.
We need to follow this map, decipher the symbols, and uncover the truth before it's too late."

Darius nodded, his gaze steady. "This quest will not be easy, Vajra. The path may lead to truths we are unprepared to face."

"Truths are better than ignorance," Vajra replied, her determination unwavering.

As they prepared to leave the chamber, Kyra held up a smaller artefact—a worn pendant etched with symbols identical to the ones on the parchment.

"This belonged to a warrior who fought to protect Kandahar centuries ago," she said softly. "Perhaps his story is tied to this mystery. Keep it with you, Vajra. It may guide you when the time comes."

Vajra took the pendant, feeling its weight in her palm. The cold metal sent a shiver through her, as if it carried the echoes of a forgotten battle.

As they exited the chamber and sealed it
once more, the whispering winds returned,
stronger now, winding through the palace like
a warning.

In her heart, Vajra knew this was only the
beginning.
Whatever they uncovered next would shape
the fate of Kandahar-and perhaps the entire
realm.

The iron door groaned as it closed, sealing
the chamber once more. The quiet that
followed was heavy, like the weight of a secret
long buried. As they made their way out of
the hidden archives, the flickering torchlight
cast long, restless shadows against the stone
walls of the palace corridors.

Vajra held the pendant tightly in her hand,
the cool metal pressing against her skin. The
engraved symbols seemed to shift under the
dim light, faint traces of something ancient
stirring within the grooves. She glanced down
at it again, feeling the inexplicable pull, as if
the pendant itself was guiding her toward
something-something she was meant to
uncover.

"I don't like this," Arian murmured beside
her, his voice low. "There's too much at stake,
too many unanswered questions. These
relics... they're more than just artefacts.
They're warnings."

"You feel it too?" Vajra's voice was a whisper,
her gaze fixed on the pendant. "This isn't just
a journey to understand the past. It's a path
we must walk to stop something from
happening. Something that could destroy us."

Kyra's voice broke through the silence, soft
but firm.
"The pendant is more than a piece of
jewellery. It was once worn by one of the last
warriors who fought to protect Kandahar
from the same shadow we face now. His
name is lost to history, but his essence is
contained in the pendant. It holds the key to
the final part of the puzzle, a hidden truth
that's been lost for centuries."

Darius, who had been quietly observing the
conversation, spoke up. "That's why we
sealed the chamber. The warriors of the past
didn't just leave these relics behind for us to
find—they left them to keep us from making
the same mistakes they did."

"But what mistakes?" Vajra pressed, her voice filled with urgency. "What happened that we're still hiding from?"

Darius exchanged a long glance with Kyra and Aryanath before answering. "The path the relics lead us on—if we follow it-may bring us closer to the enemy. But it will also bring us closer to the truth.
And the truth has a way of unraveling everything."

As they left the palace and ventured into the city streets, the sense of urgency grew. Arian unrolled the map once more, its faded edges crumbling in his hands. The symbols were still faint, barely visible against the parchment's yellowing surface, but Arian's sharp eyes caught every detail.

"The map points north," Arian said, his voice tense.

"But it's not just a direction. It's a sequence-one that we need to follow in order. Look here," he pointed to a series of lines curving toward the northern mountains. "This is the first marker. It's hidden in the cliffs—near the old ruins."

"That's where we must go," Vajra said, her voice unwavering. "But we'll need to decipher the next step along the way. The relics are connected to these locations. Each piece may hold a clue. Each marker may lead us closer to the truth."

She paused, eyes flicking back to the pendant in her hand. There was something more-something deeper
—that connected it to the symbols on the map, but she couldn't put her finger on it yet. The pendant's power seemed to pulse with an energy she couldn't fully understand. It was as if it recognised her touch, responding to some unspoken command.

"There's something about the pendant," she whispered. "It's guiding us, Arian. But I can't tell how."
Arian nodded slowly, a dark expression crossing his face. "We need to be careful. We're not the only ones looking for answers. Whoever is behind these disappearances-they know about these relics. And they'll stop at nothing to keep us from unlocking their secrets."

Vajra clenched the pendant tightly, a new resolve setting in. "Then we'll be ready for them."
The cold wind swirled around them as they made their way toward the palace gates, the shadows of the past creeping closer with each step. The map was their only guide, and the pendant their only link to a mystery that could either save or destroy Kandahar.

Chapter 4 - The Stranger at the Gates

The city of Kandahar was still, almost too still, as the sun dipped beneath the horizon, casting the streets in twilight's eerie glow. The palace gates were closed, but the sentries stood on alert, their eyes scanning the horizon as if anticipating something that had yet to arrive.

Vajra stood in the courtyard, looking out over the city. The wind was calm, but the air felt thick with tension. Arian, standing by her side, studied the map once more. The urgency in his eyes was evident.

"We can't delay much longer," he said. "We must follow the map's trail. The symbols are too important to ignore."

Vajra nodded, but just as she turned to make her way toward the palace's inner chambers

to prepare for the journey, the distant sound
of hooves reached her ears. The sentries
shifted, alert.

"Someone's coming," Darius said from
behind them.
"They're approaching the gates. Not one of
ours."
Arian's hand instinctively went to his sword
hilt. "I'll go see who it is."

But before he could take a step, the palace
gates opened, and a lone rider emerged from
the darkened road. Cloaked in black, the
figure was unrecognisable, save for the gleam
of a dagger strapped to their waist and the
strange markings on the horse's saddle—a
symbol that matched the ones on the map.

The rider slowed as they approached, their
face hidden in shadow, but there was
something unnervingly familiar about their
presence. They dismounted with practiced
ease and stood before Vajra, bowing low but
not speaking.

"Who are you?" Vajra asked, her voice
steady, yet a shiver ran down her spine.

The rider straightened, pulling back their hood to reveal a face that left her breathless- an old, forgotten face from her past.

"I have come to warn you, Princess," the stranger said, their voice quiet but laced with urgency. "The shadows are moving faster than you think. And the relics... they will lead you into more danger than you ever imagined."

Vajra's heart pounded. "Who are you? And how do you know about the relics?"

The rider paused, as if weighing the truth in their mind. Then they spoke, their words cutting through the silence like a blade.

"My name is Zarek," the stranger said. "And the relics have a power beyond what you can comprehend. But you will need them. For what's coming is darker than anything you've faced before."

The wind picked up again, carrying with it the unmistakable scent of roses-fresh, but laced with something far more sinister.

Chapter 5 - A Blade in the Shadows

The night sky above Kandahar was glimmering with stars, their soft glow shimmering against the heavy cloak of darkness that had settled over the city. The streets were quiet, save for the whispers of the wind, carrying the promise of more mysteries yet to unfold.

Arian stood in the courtyard, his mind racing through everything he had seen, everything he had heard. The relics, the symbols, Zarek's warning-they all swirled in his mind, gnawing at him. He had spent too many nights consumed by his thoughts, and tonight, the tension felt unbearable. Perhaps a walk in the city would clear his head, or so he thought.

As he wandered through the narrow, winding streets of Kandahar, the soft murmur of conversation and laughter could still be heard from the distant taverns and homes. The air was cool but pleasant, carrying with it the scent of freshly baked bread and the faint fragrance of roses that seemed to linger in every corner of the city.

Arian's footsteps slowed as he passed a dimly lit alley, where a woman emerged from the shadows. At first, he barely noticed her-just another figure in the periphery of his restless thoughts. But then, as the light caught her features, his breath caught in his chest. She was strikingly beautiful, her raven-black hair cascading down her back like a silken waterfall, her eyes as dark and mysterious as the night sky.

She didn't look lost, nor did she seem out of place.
There was a sense of quiet purpose in her movements, the grace of someone who belonged here-yet somehow, she was foreign to him.

Their gazes locked, and for a brief, suspended moment, neither of them spoke. Arian felt an inexplicable pull, something magnetic, like a fire igniting in his chest. He knew, without thinking, that this encounter was not mere coincidence.

"Good evening," she said, her voice soft but commanding, as if she had spoken these words a thousand times.

Arian found himself drawn to her, captivated by the enigmatic aura she exuded. "Evening," he replied, his voice rougher than he intended.

She stepped closer, her movements smooth, almost predatory in their precision. "You're the one who walks with shadows," she murmured, a knowing smile curving her lips. "I've seen you before, haven't I?"

Arian raised an eyebrow, unsure of what she meant.
But the allure in her voice left him momentarily speechless. "Perhaps," he replied, his curiosity piqued. "I've seen many faces in this city."

The woman laughed softly, a low, melodic sound that sent a ripple of heat through him. "Not like mine, I suspect." She stepped even closer, her scent—a mix of jasmine and something earthy-surrounding him like a fog. "I am known by many names," she continued, her fingers lightly brushing against his arm, sending sparks of electricity up his skin. "But you may call me Lira."

Arian could feel the heat rising between them, an undeniable chemistry that neither of them could ignore. His heart pounded in his chest, but it wasn't just the adrenaline of the situation—it was the intensity of her presence. Every inch of him felt alive in a way that had been dormant for too long.

"You're not just a wanderer, are you?" Arian asked, his voice dropping lower, his instincts sharpening.
"You're here for something."

Lira smiled, a wicked glint in her eyes.
"Perhaps I am.
But there's no need to rush. We have all the time in the world."

She reached up and gently cupped his face, her thumb brushing across his lips, sending a surge of desire through him. Without thinking, Arian leaned in, closing the space between them. Their lips met in a kiss that was slow at first, a gentle exploration, as though testing the waters. But soon, it deepened, more urgent, more hungry, as the fire between them flared brighter.

Time seemed to disappear in that moment. Everything outside the kiss—the city, the mission, the looming threats-faded away. It was just him and her, and the heat that was building, spreading through his veins like wildfire.

But just as the kiss reached its peak, a sharp noise cut through the air-something crashing in the distance.
Arian pulled away, his senses suddenly alert, the warmth of Lira's body still burning against his skin.

"What was that?" Arian asked, his voice tense, suddenly aware of the danger that had shifted the atmosphere.
Lira's expression hardened, her smile vanishing like mist. "It's not safe here, not anymore," she said, her tone now laced with something darker. She moved away from him, her eyes scanning the alley, before turning on her heel. "Stay alert, Arian. You'll need to."

Before he could respond, she disappeared into the shadows, as quietly as she had appeared, leaving Arian standing alone in the alley, his heart racing not just from their kiss, but from the sudden shift in the night's energy.

And then, the world erupted into chaos.

The sound of shouting reached Arian's ears, followed by the unmistakable clash of steel on steel. He ran toward the palace gates, his pulse hammering in his chest, a deep sense of dread washing over him. He reached the outer courtyard just in time to see a figure dart toward Kyra, who stood at the edge of the gathering crowd, talking to a group of soldiers.

A man in dark robes lunged from the shadows, a gleaming blade in his hand.

"No!" Arian shouted, running forward with everything he had.

But it was too late. The assassin struck, his blade cutting through the air with terrifying speed, finding its mark in Kyra's side. She gasped, her eyes wide with shock as she staggered backward, her hand instinctively clutching at the wound.

The crowd erupted in screams as guards rushed forward, but Arian was already there, pulling the assassin away from her with a forceful shove. The man's hood fell back, revealing a face Arian didn't recognise-a man

with cold, dead eyes and an expression that
seemed to be entirely devoid of remorse.

"Maaa!" Arian yelled, dropping to his knees
beside her as blood poured from the wound.
"Stay with me.
You're going to be fine.

But even as he spoke, the blood was
spreading too quickly, soaking through her
robes. Her breathing was shallow, laboured.

"I'm sorry," Kyra whispered, her voice weak
but filled with determination. "They've come.
The shadows are here, Arian. And they will
not stop..."

Arian's heart stopped as her words sank in.
The shadows. It was the same phrase Lira
had used moments earlier. The same
warning.

"What do you mean, mother?" he asked,
panic rising in his chest.

But Kyra's eyes fluttered shut, and the light in
them dimmed.

The world was falling apart...

Chapter 6 - The Council of Thorns

The early evening had descended with an eerie stillness over the palace. The air was heavy with the sense of something sinister stirring in the shadows.

Inside the grand hall, the soft murmurs of concerned soldiers filled the air, their faces drawn with exhaustion and fear. At the centre of it all stood Kyra, her posture commanding yet tempered with a mother's warmth. She was speaking with a handful of trusted soldiers, discussing their recent patrols along the outskirts of the city and the unsettling reports of increasing movement along the borders.

Whispers of enemy activity had been growing more frequent, and it was clear something larger was on the horizon.

Kyra's sharp eyes flicked between the soldiers, her voice steady yet filled with authority. "We cannot afford to underestimate what's coming," she said, her

tone piercing through the low chatter in the room.
"The enemy may be closer than we think. We need to reinforce the outer posts, ensure that our scouts are vigilant, and double-check all our defences. The city's safety depends on it."

She turned to one of the captains. "Are the secret paths still secure? Have we placed extra sentries on the northern gate?"

The captain nodded, but there was unease in his eyes. "Yes, Your Highness. But there are rumours, strange ones. People have seen shadows moving in the woods at night. I fear there's something more than just the usual skirmishes."

Kyra's gaze hardened, her lips tight with the weight of the unspoken truth. She had been worried for some time-this wasn't just about the usual border disputes. There were forces gathering, forces that would stop at nothing to claim Kandahar for themselves. And those forces had already begun their work.

As she continued to converse with the soldiers, Aryanath was in his own chambers, pouring over the ancient maps and the relics that had been uncovered in the hidden chamber. The symbols etched into the pendant seemed to shift in the dim light of his room, as if alive with meaning. Aryanath's brow furrowed in concentration as he tried to make sense of the connection between the symbols and the map.

There was a faint hum in the air, a sensation that crept along his spine, urging him to decipher the message hidden within these ancient artefacts. But no matter how much he studied, the answers eluded him, just out of reach. His frustration grew as he scribbled more notes on the parchment, but the pattern seemed incomplete.

Meanwhile, Darius was in the weapon storage compound, overseeing the readiness of the soldiers' armament. He checked the quality of their blades, their shields, ensuring that nothing was left to chance. The air in the compound was thick with the smell of iron and the sound of clanking metal. His mind, however, was not entirely on the weapons. He could feel the unease in his bones, a tension that had been growing in the air since the evening began.

Then it happened.

A scream broke through the stillness, a chilling cry that echoed across the palace grounds. Arian's voice rang out, full of panic and urgency. "Maaa!!"

Darius's heart stopped. He knew, instantly, that something was terribly wrong.

He sprinted through the compound
I, the weight of
fear pounding against his chest. When he reached the courtyard, he saw Arian holding the assassin—a figure cloaked in shadow, his face masked by darkness—his blade already wet with Kyra's blood.

In that instant, everything seemed to move in slow motion.

Kyra was crumpled on the ground, a look of shock frozen on her face. The blood soaked through her robes, staining the cobblestones.

Without a second thought, Darius ran to her, his heart breaking as he knelt by her side. "Kyra!" he shouted, shaking her gently, but she didn't respond.

Arian was struggling with the assassin. Darius tried to get out of the shock. His focus was on Kyra. He picked her up in his arms, his heart pounding, a primal need to protect her overwhelming him. He didn't care about the assassin. He didn't care about anything except getting her to safety.

"Hold on, Kyra," he whispered desperately. "Stay with me."
He carried her, running as fast as he could toward the Sushruta Ayurvedic Facility-the most trusted medical facility in Kandahar, known for its healing abilities.
As they arrived, the Vaidya—a revered healer— immediately took control, ushering them inside. "We need to stop the bleeding," the Vaidya said, her hands moving with practiced precision. "But she's losing too much blood. We must act quickly."

Arian, now free from the assassin's grasp, rushed to the facility to join them, his face drawn with concern.
He held the assassin at sword point as he was dragged in by the guards, but Arian's mind was elsewhere-on Kyra - a mother like figure from his childhood.

When Rajvanta died and his son was found guilty of helping Zarif on his money gouging motives with the enemy forces, Arian's birth mother eloped leaving her son in the palace premises. From that moment Kyra has been taking care of him as her own blood.

But now Arian was lost, as Kyra's life was hanging by a thread. He didn't want to lose his mother.

Inside the facility, the air was thick with tension. The Vaidya worked relentlessly, her eyes flicking between Kyra and the herbs she mixed, trying to stabilise her.
Darius could only stand at the doorway, his fists clenched, his breath shallow with worry. The pain in his chest was unbearable. He had been fighting for Kandahar for so long, but this-this was different.
Kyra was everything to him.

As for Aryanath, when he heard the news, it was as if the weight of the world had collapsed upon him. His chest tightened painfully, and for a moment, he couldn't breathe. His thoughts, once sharp and focused on the mystery of the symbols, were now a blur of fear and love for the woman who had been a constant in his life.
He stood frozen for a moment, the symbols now a blur before his eyes.

Kyra... He hadn't realised how deeply he cared for her until that very moment. Love had a way of transforming-growing in ways that made you understand just how much you could lose.

"She'll be fine," Aryanath whispered to himself, though even he wasn't sure he believed it. "She has to be."

Outside the facility, Vajra paced restlessly, anxiety gnawing at her. Her mother's life hung in the balance, and there was nothing she could do but wait. She hated this feeling—this helplessness that crept into her veins and tightened her chest. She wanted to protect her mother, to save her from this threat, but she knew that the road ahead would not be easy. The shadows were closing in, and every moment felt like an eternity.

As the night dragged on, Kyra's condition remained critical. The Vaidya worked tirelessly, administering herbs and treatments, trying to stop the bleeding, to stabilise her. But there was no guarantee.

Darius stood at her side, his expression grim. He had sworn to protect Kyra with his life, and now he was terrified that he would fail her. But in the depths of his soul, a fire burned brighter than ever before.

"I will not let anything happen to you, Kyra,"
he whispered through clenched teeth. "We'll
live together. We'll die together. You are my
everything."

That evening, after hours of gruelling effort,
Kyra's condition stabilised. She was not out
of danger yet, but she was alive.

Darius stood in front of the courtroom the
next day, his expression a mask of fury and
resolve. The assassin, now bound and silent,
was brought before him.

Without hesitation, Darius drew his sword
and slit the assassin's throat, the room falling
silent as the body crumpled to the floor.

"Let this be a warning to anyone who dares to
threaten my family," Darius's voice rang out,
cold and unwavering. "Anyone who thinks
they can harm those I love will find no
mercy. I will cut every throat that dares to
stand against my loved ones."

Vajra stood at the back of the room, her fists
clenched, the weight of her father's words
settling over her like a storm. She had seen
his strength before, but this-this was
something else. It was as though a new fire

had ignited within him, a fire that would consume everything in its path.

And the message was clear: The Council of Thorns had drawn its first blood, and the war was just beginning.

Chapter 7 - Across the Horizon

The days that followed Kyra's near-fatal encounter were long, filled with both hope and uncertainty. The Vaidya had worked tirelessly, and her efforts had not been in vain. Kyra's body slowly regained its strength, though her mind remained shadowed by the trauma. Every day, she would take small steps forward, the pain of the attack still lingering like an echo in her body.

Darius was by her side constantly, his presence a steady anchor as Kyra navigated the depths of her recovery. He would sit by her, speaking softly, reassuring her that the storm had passed. But even as Kyra's wounds healed, the war that loomed on the horizon was far from over. Kyra's resolve to protect Kandahar only grew stronger, her spirit tempered by the scars of the attack.

Meanwhile, Vajra's role in the city grew ever more prominent. With her mother still recovering, it was time for her to step into her leadership role fully. The diplomatic journey ahead was not one she would take lightly. It was a mission to secure alliances, to prepare Kandahar for the storm that was approaching. Vajra knew that peace could only be achieved through strength, and alliances were the key to ensuring that their future remained secure.

She gathered her closest advisors-Arian, Aryanath, and General Ashwavarna along side several trusted soldiers and sent them across the lands to forge new bonds. Her heart was heavy with the knowledge that she might not return for months. But she was resolute in her mission, knowing that the stakes had never been higher. The journey would take her to distant kingdoms, where politics and intrigue ran deep. Each step she took was a gamble, but she was ready to face the unknown.

Arian, on the other hand, was far from the diplomatic path. His mind was occupied by the brutal attack on Kyra. The assassin had been silenced, but the question of who had orchestrated the plot still lingered. It was clear now that there was a deeper conspiracy at work. Someone, or something, had set this chain of events into motion, and Arian was determined to uncover the truth.

His investigation led him deep into the heart of the city, through alleys and underground taverns where whispers of corruption and treachery filled the air.

He met with informants and spoke to those who knew the undercurrents of power. His eyes were set on the symbol that had plagued him-the one connected to the pendant Kyra had once worn. Arian could feel the weight of it pressing upon him, the connection between the attack and the symbols growing clearer by the day.

But it wasn't until he met Aryanath again, deep in the heart of the palace, that he found the breakthrough he needed. Aryanath had been poring over the map and relics for days, trying to decipher the code hidden within the ancient symbols. His fingers traced the markings, and suddenly, something clicked. The code unraveled, revealing a disturbing truth.

"The attack on your mother wasn't random," Aryanath explained quietly, his voice tense. "It's connected to the Northern Territory-the

same territory where strange disappearances
have been occurring. Villages there have
been emptied, the people gone without a
trace. And from what I can see, the symbols
were meant to point us toward something
hidden deep within those lands."

Arian's heart raced as Aryanath continued.
"This isn't just about us anymore. This is
something larger. Something that's been
building for years."

Arian's gaze shifted toward the map, and he
could feel the weight of history pressing down
upon him.
The Northern Territory had always been a
place of mystery. Rumours of ancient relics,
powerful forces hidden beneath the surface,
and the shadowy remnants of a forgotten war
had always made the region dangerous. But
now, with the symbols connected to the
Northern Territory, it seemed that the pieces
were falling into place.

As Arian began to make preparations to
investigate the Northern Territory, a familiar
figure reappeared in his life-Lira. She was a
vision of beauty, her presence striking and
magnetic, but there was something far more
dangerous beneath her allure.

She had been silent for months, and her reappearance only added to the mystery surrounding the conspiracy.
Lira approached Arian in a secluded corner of the palace garden, her eyes glinting with something both alluring and predatory. She was dressed in dark, flowing robes that barely stirred in the wind, her movements graceful but calculated. Arian had met her once before, but there had always been something elusive about her-something he couldn't quite place.

"I've been following your progress," Lira said softly, her voice a delicate whisper in the still air. "I know what you've uncovered, Arian. The Northern Territory... It's not just a place of mystery. It's the key to everything that's been happening."
Arian turned to face her, his expression cautious but intrigued. "And you know all of this because...?"

Lira smiled, the expression as enigmatic as ever.

"Let's just say I have my ways." Her fingers brushed lightly against his arm, sending a jolt of warmth through him. "But there's more, Arian. The relics, the symbols... they all tie together. And I can help you find them. But in return, I need something from you."

Her gaze locked with his, and for a moment, the world seemed to fall away. "What is it that you want?" Arian asked, his voice lower now, a hint of vulnerability in his tone.

"I want to see the hidden relics," she replied softly.
"The ones you've been keeping secret. The ones tied to your people's past. I need to understand them... for reasons of my own."

Arian hesitated. His instincts screamed at him to walk away, to not trust her, but there was something in her eyes-something that stirred a long-forgotten fire within him. It wasn't just the mystery of her; it was the undeniable pull between them, the chemistry that simmered beneath the surface.
He took a deep breath, his mind racing. He knew he should say no. He knew he should keep the relics hidden. But when she stepped closer, when her breath mingled with his, when her lips brushed lightly against his ear, he could no longer resist.

Before he knew it, her hands were on his chest, her body pressing against his as their lips met in a fiery kiss. The heat between them was instant, undeniable.

It was as if all the air had been sucked from the space around them, leaving only the thudding of their hearts and the rush of blood in their veins. The kiss deepened, passionate and raw, their bodies responding to the hunger that neither could deny.

Lira's hands roamed, her fingers tracing the line of his jaw, pulling him closer, as if she wanted to consume him completely. The world outside ceased to exist-there was only the intensity of the moment, the rising heat between them, their bodies trembling with desire.

Just as quickly as it had begun, Lira pulled away, her lips brushing against his once more, this time softer, slower. She looked into his eyes with a knowing smile.

"You don't have to decide now," she whispered. "But when the time comes, Arian, you'll have to trust me. I can help you... but only if you're willing to let go of the past."

Her words lingered in the air as she turned and disappeared into the shadows, leaving Arian standing there, breathless and torn. The weight of the decision he had to make pressed down on him, but one thing was clear: the path ahead was fraught with danger, and Lira was no longer just a mystery.

She was a part of it.

As Arian stood alone in the garden, his mind a whirlwind of questions, one truth remained at the forefront of his thoughts: the journey ahead was more dangerous than he had ever imagined. The relics, the secrets of the Northern Territory, the symbols-everything was connected, and nothing would ever be the same again.

The stage was set. The players had all taken their positions. And across the horizon, a storm was brewing.

Chapter 8 - The Prince of Dusk

The court of Begram was shining with the weight of power and intrigue. The grand hall shimmered with the opulence of Greek and Indian artistry combined
—a marriage of cultures that bore the mark of centuries of conquest and assimilation. At the centre of it all sat Menander, the Prince of Dusk, a figure as enigmatic as the stars themselves.

Born to a lineage of Greek settlers in the Kabul Valley, Menander had inherited not just his ancestor's cunning but also their charm. His upbringing in Begram, a city of trade and knowledge, had shaped him into a man of profound intellect and magnetic charisma.

With a face that bore the sharp, chiseled features of his Greek forebears and eyes as piercing as the edge of a blade, he had

48

become a leader whose presence commanded both fear and admiration.

Menander was a man of contrasts - his sharp military acumen was matched only by his love for art, literature, and debate. Though he led the enemy faction, tales of his fairness and wisdom had reached even the ears of Kandahar. Some whispered that Menander sought not just power but a dream of unity, a vision of a world where cultures could coexist rather than clash.

Meanwhile, Vajra's diplomatic journey had taken her to the edge of the Kabul Valley, where tensions with Menander's forces had escalated. She had not anticipated an encounter with the enigmatic prince, but fate had other plans.

One evening, as her delegation camped near the borderlands, a summons arrived. The messenger, clad in the distinct armour of Menander's soldiers, carried an invitation to the court of Begram. The message was both a challenge and a test—a meeting between two powers, each trying to gauge the other's intentions.

Vajra, always bold and unflinching, decided to accept.

Begram stood like a crown jewel amid the rugged landscape of the Kabul Valley, a city of shimmering domes and grand colonnades.

The streets were lined with marble statues of Greek gods, blending seamlessly with Indian carvings of deities. At the city's heart, vibrant bazaars bustled with traders from far-off lands, their goods a kaleidoscope of colours and scents-spices, silk, and rare jewels. The air was alive with music, laughter, and the distant hum of philosophical debates in public forums.

As Vajra entered the city gates, she couldn't help but notice the stark differences between Begram and Kandahar. Where Kandahar celebrated its rugged simplicity and harmony with the surrounding desert, Begram boasted a proud, almost ostentatious display of its wealth and culture. The people of Begram moved with an air of cosmopolitan sophistication, their attire an elegant blend of Greek togas and Indian drapes. The city felt both alien and alluring, a place where ideas and traditions collided to create something entirely unique.

For Vajra, the sight was fascinating, but it also carried an undercurrent of unease. This was a world unlike her own, one that seemed to

prioritise power and grandeur over the quiet
resilience she cherished in Kandahar.
The court of Begram buzzed with
anticipation as Vajra entered, her presence
commanding attention.

Dressed in the ceremonial garb of Kandahar,
she stood tall, her poise and confidence
unshaken by the dozens of curious eyes fixed
upon her.

At the far end of the hall, Menander rose
from his throne. The moment their eyes met,
the energy in the room shifted. Menander's
gaze lingered on Vajra, taking in her fierce
beauty and the unmistakable fire in her eyes.
She was unlike any woman he had ever
encountered- proud, unyielding, and radiant
with the power of a leader.

"Welcome, Princess Vajra," Menander said,
his voice smooth and rich, like honey laced
with steel. "It is not often that I have the
honour of meeting someone whose
reputation precedes them so thoroughly."

Vajra inclined her head, her tone measured.
"The honour is mutual, Prince Menander.
I've heard much of your wisdom and
strength-qualities I hope are reflected in your
intentions for this meeting."

Menander chuckled, the sound warm and
genuine.
"Straight to the point. I admire that." He
gestured for her to join him at a smaller table
away from the throne, where wine and
delicacies had been laid out.

Their conversation began formally, each
testing the other with subtle words and veiled
intentions.
Menander spoke of his people's hardships, of
the struggles faced by those caught between
cultures.
Vajra countered with stories of Kandahar's
resilience, emphasising the strength of her
people and their will to protect their
homeland.

But as the evening wore on, the formality
began to slip away. They found themselves
drawn to each other-not just as leaders but as
kindred spirits.

Vajra's sharp intellect and wit matched
Menander's charm, and their banter carried a
spark that neither could ignore.

At one point, Menander leaned in slightly,
his voice dropping to a softer tone. "Tell me,
Princess... do you ever tire of the weight of

leadership? Of carrying the hopes and dreams of so many on your shoulders?"

Vajra hesitated for a moment, his question catching her off guard. "I do," she admitted, her voice quieter now. "But it's a burden I embrace. My people deserve nothing less."

Menander studied her for a long moment, a faint smile playing on his lips. "You're remarkable," he said simply.
Vajra's heart skipped a beat, but she quickly masked her reaction. "Flattery will get you nowhere, Prince," she replied, though the faintest smile touched her lips.

As the night deepened, their conversation turned to more personal matters. Vajra found herself intrigued by Menander's dreams of unity, even as she questioned his methods.

He, in turn, was captivated by her passion and resolve, qualities that made her unlike anyone he had ever met.
But the moment was not to last. As Vajra prepared to leave, Menander stepped closer, his expression unreadable.

"I hope this won't be the last time we meet, Princess," he said softly.

"That depends on the choices you make, Prince," Vajra replied, her tone half-teasing, half-serious.

Then, with a bow, Vajra turned and left, her heart conflicted.

Back at the camp, Arian was restless. The attack on Kyra still haunted him, and his investigation had yielded little progress. But as he poured over the symbols late into the night, a realisation struck him.
The patterns on the map and pendant were not random-they pointed to Begram.

When he shared his findings with Aryanath, the elder advisor's expression turned grim.
"It seems our enemy isn't just in the shadows," Aryanath said. "The Prince of Begram may hold the key to unraveling this mystery."

Arian's thoughts turned dark. If Menander was involved, then Vajra was walking into a den of vipers.
Meanwhile, in the shadowed corridors of the Northern Territory, Lira was moving with purpose.

The desolate villages had left her uneasy, and the lack of answers weighed on her mind.

The mystery of the disappearances was growing more troubling by the day. But there was more to Lira's mission than simply investigating the villages.

Lira was no ordinary wanderer-she was born in Begram, a daughter of its elite warrior caste.
Her piercing beauty and razor-sharp mind had earned her a place in Menander's inner circle, and she now held a high rank in his army. A trusted agent of Begram, Lira had built a reputation as a brilliant strategist and a deadly combatant.

But she was more than just a soldier. Lira was a master of secrets, a woman whose true allegiances were known only to herself.

Though her loyalty seemed to lie with Begram, her presence in Kandahar raised troubling questions.
Was she merely gathering intelligence for Menander, or did she have her own agenda?

As Lira returned to Begram that evening, her path crossed with Menander's in one of the palace's quieter halls.

"You're late," Menander said, his tone light but edged with curiosity.

"Trouble in the Northern Territory," Lira replied, her voice as calm and measured as always.

She hesitated for a moment before adding, "The villages are empty, Menander. This is bigger than we thought."

Menander frowned, his mind racing with possibilities. "Do you believe the Kandaharis are behind it?"

Lira's lips curved into a faint smile, though her eyes remained unreadable. "Perhaps. Or perhaps someone wants us to think they are.

Either way, it's a dangerous game."
Menander studied her for a long moment, his gaze piercing. Lira was one of the few people he truly trusted, but even he could not entirely decipher her.
Their shared history bound them together in ways neither could ignore.

"Be careful, Lira," he said finally. "I need you alive more than ever."

Her smile widened, though it carried a hint of something darker. "Always."

Menander was standing on the balcony of his palace, gazing out at the horizon where Kandahar lay. The spark between him and Vajra was undeniable, but so too were the shadows gathering around them.

"She'll change everything," Menander murmured to himself, his voice low. "But for better or worse... I cannot say."

Chapter 9 - Fire Beneath the Sand

The desert wind howled against the silent expanse, its whisper carrying secrets buried deep beneath the golden sands. The moon hung low over the Kandahar outpost where Arian paced restlessly in his quarters.

A knock at the door broke his reverie. When he opened it, there stood Lira, bathed in the soft glow of the lanterns outside. Her presence was magnetic— her piercing eyes holding secrets he didn't yet know he needed, her beauty dangerous and alluring.

"We need to talk," she said, stepping inside without waiting for permission. The sway of her movements spoke of confidence, but her voice held a rare trace of urgency.

"Lira."

Arian said, his brow furrowing, "What are you
hiding from me?"

Lira met his gaze, her demeanour cool and composed.
"This isn't about what I'm hiding, Arian. It's about what you need to know."
She pulled a small scroll from the folds of her cloak and unfurled it on the table. It was an old map of Kandahar, marked with the same symbols Aryanath had been deciphering. But beside the symbols were scribbled notes—names, dates, locations.

"These are the places Zarif frequented," Lira began.

"He wasn't just passing secrets between Kandahar and Begram—he was also trying to protect someone.

"Who", he asked
"His brother."

Arian's breath caught. "What are you saying?"

Lira stepped closer, her voice dropping to a conspiratorial whisper. "Your father helped Zarif.
Not out of greed or betrayal, but to save him. Zarif's brother was being held in Begram's custody, and they forced Zarif to spy on Kandahar in exchange for his brother's life. Your father knew this. He tried to help Zarif by keeping the information under wraps. But things spiralled out of control when Zarif began giving false intelligence to Darius to protect his brother."
Arian felt his chest tighten. "But Zarif... he was caught, wasn't he? My father never said anything— he just vanished. My mother wouldn't even tell me why."

"Because they didn't have a choice," Lira said sharply. "Darius saw Zarif as a traitor, and when your father tried to explain, Darius refused to listen.
He's a man who only believes what he sees. Your father kept silent to save your family from the fallout, but it cost him everything. Your mother has been living in the shadows ever since."

Arian staggered back, the weight of her words hitting him like a blow. His entire world felt as though it was crumbling beneath him. The father he had long believed was a traitor...

wasn't. And now his mother was tied to secrets he could barely comprehend.

"Why are you telling me this now?" Arian demanded, his voice breaking.

"Because the truth has a way of surfacing when it's least convenient," Lira said. "And because you deserve to know what really happened. But Arian," she added, her voice softening, "if you go after this, if you try to free Zarif and your father... you'll set off a political storm that will tear Kandahar apart."

Arian clenched his fists. "Then let it. My family deserves justice."

Lira sighed, stepping closer. Her hand lightly grazed his arm, and the contact sent a spark through him.
"You don't understand. Darius is adamant. He doesn't listen to reason, and if you push him on this, you'll risk not just your father's life, but your own."

Arian turned to her, his emotions a storm of anger, heartbreak, and confusion. "Why are you telling me all this? What do you gain from it?"

Lira's lips curved into a faint, enigmatic smile. "I told you—I knew your birth mother. She was a friend to me once. I owe her this much."

The tension between them grew thick in the silence that followed, their words giving way to a shared understanding. Arian's gaze lingered on Lira, her beauty more striking in the soft glow of the lantern light. Her sharp edges and piercing wit hid a vulnerability he rarely glimpsed, and in that moment, he was drawn to her like a moth to flame.

"Why are you helping me, really?" he asked, his voice quieter now.

Lira stepped closer, her breath warm against his neck. "Maybe I see something in you," she whispered, her voice a mix of danger and allure. "Or maybe I just can't stay away."

Arian didn't have time to respond before her lips met his. The kiss was slow at first, a testing of boundaries, but it quickly deepened. Her hands slid over his shoulders, pulling him closer as his own fingers trailed down the curve of her back. The heat between them built like wildfire, their breaths growing heavier as they gave in to the moment.

Lira's cloak fell to the floor, revealing the toned body of a warrior. Arian's hands explored her skin, tracing the lines of old scars that told a story of battles won and lost. She pulled him closer, their bodies pressed together as the tension between them ignited into something fierce and consuming.

They fell back onto the carpet in the corner of the room, the world outside forgotten. Arian's fingers slid through her hair as she leaned into him, their kisses growing more urgent and fevered. The heat of the desert seemed to seep into the room, making every touch, every breath feel electric.

As their breaths mingled and the room became a cocoon of unspoken desires, Lira's beauty radiated like the soft glow of a flame. Her body, sculpted with precision from years of discipline and battle, was mesmerising. Every inch of her skin seemed to tell a story- one of resilience, allure, and untamed power.

Arian traced the curve of her shoulders with his fingertips, marvelling at how her strength was matched by a softness that only deepened her beauty.

Her chest rose and fell beneath the thick silk cloth draped over her, her breaths quickening as his lips brushed her neck.

His kisses grew bolder, trailing down the delicate line of her back, where he paused. Slowly, he brought his mouth to the knot of the silk cloth, his teeth carefully undoing it.

The fabric loosened, slipping away to reveal her bare skin, shimmering with the glow of lantern light. She shivered slightly as his lips pressed against the small of her back, his embrace pulling her closer.

Turning her gently toward him, Arian let his hands glide over her arms, his touch reverent yet urgent.
His lips found her navel, lingering there before traveling upward to her hand, her shoulder, and finally the curve of her chest. Lira's breath hitched as his kisses deepened, and a quiet moan escaped her lips. The sound, raw and unguarded, ignited something primal between them.

Lira pressed herself against him, her hands tangling in his hair as their kisses became hungrier, their bodies melting into one another. The pulse of the moment grew more intense, and she arched beneath his

touch, her moans growing louder, echoing
softly against the walls.

Their bodies moved together, a rhythm
forged from passion and unspoken emotion.
Beads of sweat formed on their skin, the heat
of the moment overwhelming, yet neither
wanted to stop. Arian held her close, his
hands tracing the contours of her back, her
hips, her thighs.

As the moment reached its peak, Lira
gasped, her moans muffled as she buried her
face against his neck. Arian's own voice broke
through in a deep breath with a harsh moan,
as if he roared.

Holding her close, he pressed his forehead
against her neck, their breaths mingling as
they came back to earth together.
The room was silent but for the sound of
their breathing, their bodies still entwined,
glistening with the sweat of their passion.

Arian tightened his hold on her, as if afraid to
let go.
Lira's fingers traced patterns along his chest,
her expression softening into something
vulnerable, a stark contrast to her usual sharp
confidence.

But even as the fire between them simmered into a quiet glow, a shadow hung in the air — unspoken truths, buried secrets, and the knowledge that their moment of closeness would not shield them from the storms yet to come.

"You can't tell anyone about this," Lira said, her voice soft but firm.
Arian turned to her, his brow furrowing. "About us?"
"No," she replied, her eyes darkening. "About the relics. About what we know. If Darius finds out...
.."
She trailed off, her voice heavy with unspoken warnings.

Arian's jaw tightened. "I don't care what Darius thinks. He doesn't scare me."

"He should," Lira said, sitting up and reaching for her cloak. "Because if you go down this path, Arian, you'll be walking through fire. And not everyone survives the flames.'

With that, she slipped out of the room, leaving Arian alone with his thoughts. But her scent lingered, a mix of sandalwood and danger, and the memory of her touch burned into his skin.

In the shadowed halls of Begram, Lira made
her way back to Menander's private quarters.
Her face was a mask of composure, but her
heart raced with the weight of the choices she
had made.

Menander was waiting for her, his expression
unreadable. "Did you find what you were
looking for?" he asked, his voice low.

Lira hesitated for only a moment before
nodding. "I did. But this isn't over."

"No," Menander agreed, his gaze piercing.
"It's just beginning."

Menander stands there staring out over the
sands of the Kabul Valley, the fire of conflict
glowing faintly on the horizon.

The journey north was gruelling, an endless expanse of dust and shadows swallowing the daylight. Arian rode in silence, his thoughts in turmoil as the path unraveled before them. Lira was close beside him, her steady presence an unspoken reassurance. Yet, the weight of what they were seeking-disappeared villagers,
 mysterious symbols, Zarif's secrets-hung heavy between them, unspoken but ever present.

As night fell, they reached the boundary of the Northern Territory. The land here was uncanny, as though it belonged to another world. Gnarled trees clung to dry earth, their twisted branches clawing at the sky. Faint whispers rose on the wind, voices that seemed to emerge from nowhere. The ruins of the village lay before them—an expanse of crumbled homes, broken wells, and silence that pressed in like a shroud.

Lira dismounted first, her eyes scanning the
area.
Arian followed suit, his sword half-drawn as
he scanned the ruins.
"This place feels..." Lira trailed off, searching
for the word.

"Haunted," Arian finished, his voice low.

The air shifted then, sharp and cold. It was
subtle at first—a whisper carried on the wind,
faint and fleeting. Then it came again, clearer
this time.

"Arian...

The sound froze him in place. The voice was
soft, unmistakably familiar, and it reached
into a part of him he'd thought long buried.
He turned sharply, his breath catching as a
figure emerged from the shadows of a
shattered archway.

She moved like a ghost-cautious, hesitant-her
tattered cloak blending into the twilight. For a
long moment, she remained hidden beneath
the hood, as though afraid to reveal herself.
Then, with trembling hands, she pushed it
back.

Arian staggered back a step, the air rushing from his lungs.

The woman before him was older than he remembered, her face etched with lines of sorrow and survival. But her eyes... her eyes were his own.
"Mother," he choked out.

Her lip quivered, tears brimming as she took a step forward. "My son," she whispered. "My Arian."

Arian felt the world tilt beneath his feet. Lira said nothing but stepped back to give them space, though her watchful gaze never strayed far.

"You..." Arian swallowed hard, his voice breaking.
"You were dead. They told me you were dead."
"I know," she said softly. "I know what they told you.
And I wanted you to believe it."

The words struck him like a blow. "What do you mean?"

"I had to disappear, Arian. For you. For your survival."

Arian's hands clenched at his sides. The anger rose like bile in his throat, tangled with the disbelief and pain of seeing her alive. "You left me. I mourned you.

I needed you."

Her shoulders shook with the weight of his words.
She stepped forward slowly, as though approaching a wounded animal. "I know, my son. And I will never forgive myself for what I did. But listen to me. There was no other way."

He looked away, his jaw tight. "Where have you been? All these years?"

She exhaled shakily, as though the memories themselves were too heavy to bear. "They took me-men under Darius' orders. I was... I was a means to an end for him."

At the mention of Darius, Arian's gaze snapped back to her. "Darius?"

"Yes," she said bitterly, her voice thick with disdain.
"His hunger for power-his obsession with Kandahar's secrets-knew no limits. I knew things, Arian. Your father..." She paused,

closing her eyes for a brief moment. "Your father's bloodline is connected to the symbols you've been chasing. They're more than carvings. They're ancient seals meant to bind an old darkness. Darius wanted control of that power, and he believed I knew the key."

Arian staggered, the words sinking in slowly. "My father..?"
She nodded. "He belonged to a lineage sworn to protect those seals, to ensure the darkness beneath the sands would remain imprisoned. But Darius was relentless. When I refused to help him, he made sure I vanished. He knew if I stayed near you, you would one day learn the truth."

Lira, who had been silent until now, finally spoke.
Her voice was calm but sharp. "And the villagers?
The ones who disappeared?"

Arian's mother turned toward her, her expression pained. "They were caught in the storm Darius began. The seals in this land are weakening, Lira.
With every breach, the darkness grows stronger. The villagers... they were either taken by it or consumed."

The words hung in the air, chilling Arian to
his core.
He looked at his mother, his voice unsteady.
"Why didn't you come back for me?"

Tears slipped down her cheeks now, though
her voice remained steady. "I couldn't. Darius
kept me hidden, and by the time I escaped, I
had no way of knowing where you were. I
thought if I returned, it would only put you in
danger. So I stayed here, watching, waiting.
And now you've come."

Arian stared at her, every emotion crashing
over him
-grief, anger, longing, and an aching love he
hadn't allowed himself to feel in years. "I
needed you," he whispered again, his voice
breaking.

She stepped closer, her hand trembling as
she reached up to touch his face. "And I
needed you, Arian. You are all I have left."

For the first time, Arian allowed himself to let
go. He closed his eyes as tears traced down
his cheeks, the years of pain pouring out of
him.

Lira turned away then, giving them the privacy they deserved. But her mind raced with everything she had heard.

Finally, Arian's mother straightened, the steel returning to her gaze. "This darkness will not stop, Arian. If the seals are broken, Kandahar-and all who live in its shadow-will fall."

Arian wiped his face, his resolve hardening. "Then we stop it. Tell me where to begin."

She nodded, her face grave. "Beneath the sands. The fire sleeps in the place where the first seal was forged."
Lira rejoined them then, her gaze lingering on Arian.
"Are you ready for this?"

Arian looked between his mother and Lira, the weight of their task settling on his shoulders. "I don't have a choice."

His mother's voice lowered, barely above a whisper.
"But be warned, Arian. There are forces in this land that do not wish to be forgotten. They will fight to stay free."

The wind picked up then, shrill and unearthly, carrying with it an eerie sound—a whisper, like voices rising from the earth itself. Lira stepped closer to Arian, her fingers brushing against his arm as though to steady him.

In the distance, shadows flickered at the edge of their vision, darting between the broken trees. And in that moment, Arian understood: whatever darkness lay beneath the sand was already awake.

And it was watching them.

Chapter 11 - The Siege of Bloodstone Keep

The Northern Territory stretched out in a vast, oppressive silence as Arian, Lira, and his mother pressed deeper into its heart. Beneath a leaden sky, the ground seemed to breathe unease. The ruins of the village gave way to jagged cliffs, beyond which lay Bloodstone Keep, a long-abandoned fortress that loomed against the horizon like a scar left by forgotten wars.

Arian's mother stopped abruptly as the keep came into view. Her voice trembled as she whispered,
"This is where it began."

Lira glanced at Arian, her brows furrowed. Arian nodded, his gaze fixed on the weather-worn stones of the keep. "This is where Darius left his mark. He's been here."

His mother's voice was low, her words drenched in foreboding. "Bloodstone Keep was a village once, built around that fortress. A place of simple people who sought refuge from the desert's cruelty. But Darius... he destroyed it."

"Why?" Arian asked, his tone edged with suspicion and urgency. "What was he looking for here?"

She didn't answer immediately. Her gaze was distant, as if the echoes of the past were whispering only to her. "Power. Secrets. And a key to darkness no mortal should wield."

Arian's jaw tightened. "Show me."

Together, they crossed the dry plains leading to the keep. Each step felt heavier than the last, as though the land itself resented their presence. The great gates had long since fallen, reduced to splintered wood and rusted iron. Inside, the remnants of what had once been a bustling village were scattered — shattered pottery, torn cloth, blackened stone where fires had burned too hot.

The walls seemed to whisper as they moved through the ruins, their footsteps echoing. Lira broke the silence, her voice barely above a whisper. "What happened here?"

"It was a siege," Arian's mother said, her tone brittle.
"The villagers never stood a chance. Darius' forces came at night, swift and merciless."

And *she continued to explain...*

Suddenly, Arian stopped mid-step, his breath hitching. The air shimmered in front of him, a distortion like heat rising off a sun-scorched road.

Then, as though some unseen veil had been lifted, he saw it-flashes.

The Siege

The night was alive with screams. Fires raged as shadows moved like predators through the streets, blades flashing in the moonlight. Arian saw men and women fleeing, their faces twisted in terror as Darius' soldiers cut them down without hesitation.

Through the haze of smoke, he saw a rider—a lone horseman-charging through the chaos, shouting orders to rally the villagers. His voice was desperate, commanding, until-Darius appeared, a dark silhouette against the flames. His presence froze the world. Arian saw him step forward with a measured calm, as though the carnage around him was merely a play for his amusement. The horseman reined his horse to a halt, his eyes narrowing as he turned his blade toward Darius.

"You'll find no power here," the rider spat, his voice strong even in the face of death.

Darius tilted his head, his expression devoid of emotion. "Power is everywhere if you know where to look."

Before the rider could respond, Darius lunged. With inhuman precision, he drove his sword upward into the horseman's throat. The blade erupted through the back of his skull, glistening red in the firelight.

The horse reared, shrieking as its rider crumpled lifelessly to the ground.

The vision hit Arian like a physical blow, the shock dragging him back to the present. His hand flew to his chest as he gasped for air, sweat beading on his brow. Lira was instantly at his side, her voice sharp with concern.

"Arian! What is it?"

He staggered forward, clutching the
crumbling stone of a nearby wall for support.
"I saw it."

"Saw what?" Lira demanded.

"The siege. Darius was here." His voice was
ragged, haunted. "He led the attack. He killed
the rider."

His mother watched him closely, her eyes full
of both sorrow and knowing. "The rider was
the last to resist him. His death sealed the
fate of this place."

Arian turned to her sharply. "Why? Why did
he come here? What was he after?"

She hesitated, the shadows of her past
reflected in her gaze. "The keep holds
something hidden—a piece of the truth he's
been chasing for years. He didn't want the
villagers; he wanted what they protected."

Lira stepped forward, her voice hard. "What
truth?
What did Darius know?"

"The symbols," Arian's mother replied softly.
"The ancient seals that hold the darkness

beneath this land. Bloodstone Keep was built atop one of them.
The villagers were the keepers of the seal, though most of them didn't know it. Darius needed to shatter the protection to get closer to whatever lies beneath."

The pieces were falling into place in Arian's mind, the threads of the mystery twisting tighter with every word. "He slaughtered them all to break the seal. But why? What does he want with the darkness?"

Lira's voice grew quieter, edged with suspicion.
"Perhaps he believes he can control it."

Arian's mother shook her head. "No one can control it. The darkness beneath the sands isn't meant to be touched. It's older than kingdoms and men. It corrupts everything it touches."

Arian's mind burned with questions, but one stuck out above the rest. "How do you know all of this?"

She looked at him then, her gaze deep and sorrowful.

"Because Darius used me to find it. He thought I could help him, that I had answers. I didn't. But in his madness, he kept me alive, trying to force me to reveal secrets I didn't know. He believed that by breaking the seals, he would unlock power beyond imagining. And Bloodstone Keep was his first step."

Arian's fists clenched as the rage boiled in his chest.

"He destroyed all of this-for power."

Lira placed a hand on his arm, grounding him. "What matters now is stopping him, Arian."

Arian turned, his gaze dark with determination.

"We're not leaving here until we find every trace of what he did. If there's anything left-anything that tells us what Darius is planning—we'll find it."

They searched the ruins for hours, combing through ash and rubble. At the base of the fortress, they found it—a stone chamber, hidden beneath layers of collapsed walls. The air inside was heavy, choked with an unnatural stillness.

On the far wall, Arian saw it: a symbol carved
deep into the stone, identical to those Zarif
had been tracing. But this one was broken,
the lines fractured as though something had
forced its way through.

Blood-long dried-streaked the floor beneath
it.
"This is where it happened," Lira whispered,
her
voice a breath in the cold air.

Arian stared at the broken seal, his heart
pounding.
He could almost hear the echoes of Darius'
voice in his mind, the arrogance, the
certainty.

And then he saw it-just a glimmer—a faint,
glowing crack within the stone, as though
something waited on the other side.

Arian's voice was low, full of dread. "He
didn't just break the seal. He released
something."

Lira and his mother looked at him, their
faces pale.
The whispers on the wind grew louder then,
rising from the cracks in the earth-soft,
ancient, and hungry.

And for the first time, Arian understood the true depth of what Darius had done.

Whatever lay beneath the sands was no longer sleeping.
And it was calling to him.

Chapter 12 - The Betrayal of the Wolf

The wind tore through the desolate plains of
the Northern Territory, carrying with it the
weight of a forgotten history. As Arian sat
near the dying embers of the campfire, the
memory of Aryanath's words returned to him
like a whisper across time.

"The Prince of Begram may hold the key to
unraveling this mystery. It seems our enemy
isn't just in the shadows."

Those words had lingered in his mind,
gnawing at his thoughts like a predator
circling its prey. He knew Aryanath had been
right - Begram's hand was bloodied in this
just as much as Kandahar's. And now, as he
looked at the worn maps spread across the
ground, the truth became unavoidable.

Beside him, Lira studied the lines carved into the brittle parchment. Arian's mother stood further back, her gaze fixed on the vast stretch of nothingness that had once been thriving villages.
"This land has been torn apart," Lira murmured, tracing a finger along the trade routes marked in faded ink. "So much blood spilled... and for what?"

Arian's voice was quiet, but filled with an edge of bitterness. "For power. Kandahar and Begram have always shared a common interest in the Northern Territory-until they didn't. When the land was divided, it was easier to exploit. The kings encouraged its fragmentation because it kept the villages weak and the profits strong."

His mother turned to face them, her eyes clouded with memories. "It's more than trade, Arian. This land is the spine of the world. Control its routes, and you hold the pulse of every kingdom's wealth.

Begram and Kandahar both knew it. The spices, the silks, the oils-everything that kingdoms crave flows from this region. That is why they bled it dry."

"And now Darius wants it all," Lira added, her voice sharp.

Arian nodded, his gaze fixed on the map. "He isn't content with scraps or alliances. He wants to take the Northern Territory and claim it under his rule. If he succeeds, he'll have a monopoly over the trade routes. With that power, Kandahar won't just be a kingdom—it will be an empire. The merchants will bow to him, and every ruler will depend on him to keep their people fed and clothed."

His mother's voice trembled slightly. "And he'll stop at nothing to make it so."

The words hung in the air like smoke, their weight pressing down on all three of them. Arian looked up at the dark horizon, his thoughts spiralling toward the ruins of Bloodstone Keep and the horrors he'd seen in his vision.

"He destroyed Bloodstone Keep for a reason," Arian said, his tone grave. "The siege wasn't just about sending a message. He was looking for something— something beneath the sands. A key to whatever darkness lies hidden here. But he wouldn't stop there."

Lira's brow furrowed. "You think there's more?"

"I know there's more," Arian replied. "This land isn't just valuable for its trade. There's power here— ancient power-and Darius has been chasing it for years. If he finds it, no army will stop him."

His mother's voice broke the silence, carrying with it a quiet sorrow. "I've seen his madness, Arian. When I was his prisoner, he spoke of the Northern Territory as though it belonged to him already. But he's not just a conqueror-he's something darker. He doesn't just want power. He wants dominion."

The fire crackled softly as Lira leaned closer, her voice low. "And Menander? The Prince of Begram won't stand idly by while Darius seizes control of the trade routes."

"No," Arian agreed, his gaze hardening. "But Menander is no better. Begram has its own interests here. They've propped up warlords and sowed division in these lands for decades, playing the villages against one another while profiting from their chaos. The only difference is that Begram didn't have the ambition-or perhaps the ruthlessness-to seize the land outright."

Lira looked at him, her eyes sharp with understanding. "But now Menander might be cornered. If Darius takes the Northern Territory, Begram's power crumbles."

Arian met her gaze. "Exactly. Menander has no choice but to act, and that makes him dangerous.
He's a wolf pretending to wear a crown, and he'll bare his teeth the moment he sees an opportunity."
The wind picked up, sweeping through the camp with a haunting cry, as if the land itself remembered all the blood that had been spilled upon it.

"We need to know what Menander is planning," Arian said after a long pause. "If he knows anything about Darius' motives, or if he's plotting something of his own, we can't afford to be blind to it."

Lira nodded, her expression resolute. "So what's our next move?"

Arian stood slowly, his shadow stretching long across the ground. "We're going to Begram. I'll speak with Menander myself. He's hiding something, and I intend to uncover it."

Lira raised an eyebrow, a faint smirk tugging at her lips. "And you think he'll just hand you the truth?"

"No," Arian replied darkly. "But Menander likes to play games. And I'm tired of playing blind."

His mother's voice broke through, soft but steady. "Be careful, Arian. Menander may not be Darius, but he's still a king. And kings are not to be trusted."

Arian's gaze was distant, already focused on what lay ahead. "Trust has nothing to do with it. Lira will return to Kabul. Vajra, and I will ride for Begram at first light. Mother will stay in the safe house near Kabul. And Lira, from there you join us later right after we meet the Prince. He must not know anything about our common motives.. If the Crown Prince holds answers, we'll find them."

"And if he doesn't?" Lira asked quietly.

"Then we'll look for the truth elsewhere," Arian said, his tone hard as stone. "But I'll find out what Darius is hiding—one way or another."

The night settled heavily over the camp, the
wind whispering secrets that had been buried
for generations. As Arian stared out into the
darkness, he couldn't shake the feeling that
the land itself was watching, waiting.
Somewhere beyond the walls of Begram,
Darius' shadow stretched long and deep, and
the answers Arian sought lay hidden within its
depths.

But there was something else too-something
Darius would never tell him, something even
darker than conquest and power.

And as the fire burned low, Arian swore to
himself that he would uncover it, sooner or
later!

Chapter 13 - Ties of the Past

Arian rode hard through the dense woods, the wind whipping against his face as if urging him forward.
The rhythmic pounding of his horse's hooves matched the storm of questions raging in his mind.

He had left Lira and his mother safely behind in the Kabul corridor, trusting they would make their way to a secure shelter. But his own path led straight to Kandahar—a place where answers awaited him.

The image of the symbol haunted him. The jagged lines, the spiral chaos... its meaning twisted in his mind like a snake coiling tighter with every thought.

He recalled Ashwavarna's grim voice and Vajra's unease when they had first seen it.

"Linked to an ancient sect. A forgotten
faction that once sought to tear Kandahar
apart." The words lingered in his ears like an
omen.
As Kandahar's great gates rose into view
against the dusky sky, Arian slowed his horse,
his knuckles pale from gripping the reins too
tightly. The guards saluted him with respect,
though he barely noticed.
His mind was already on what needed to be
done.

Minutes later, he entered the grand hall
where Aryanath was waiting. The elder
warrior looked up from a pile of ancient
scrolls scattered across the table, his sharp
gaze meeting Arian's.

"You came sooner than expected," Aryanath
said, setting aside a parchment. "I take it the
journey was eventful?"

"It was," Arian replied tersely. He turned to
the aide at the door. "Summon Commander
Ashwavarna immediately."

Ashwavarna was the great grandson of Old
Bhadrasen and one of the most trusted and
loyal warrior in Kandahar's army.

The aide scurried away, leaving the two men in silence. Aryanath studied Arian carefully. "You're troubled."

"Wouldn't you be?" Arian shot back, pacing to the edge of the room. "If King Darius, I mean Father has been active in the Northern Territory, why didn't Commander Ashwavarna know about the massacres? Why hasn't anyone raised their voice?"
Aryanath sighed, his expression shadowed. "Because fear silences men. That land is chaos, Arian. It's been left broken for too long, and now it's as if it devours its own people."

Before Arian could respond, the door creaked open and Commander Ashwavarna entered, his armour faintly dusted with sand. He saluted, then faced Arian. "You summoned me, my lord?"

Arian wasted no time. "Is there anything you need to tell me? Anything I don't know? I'm a warrior in Kandahar's army—I deserve the truth."

Ashwavarna's jaw tightened. For a moment, the hall seemed to hold its breath before he spoke. "When we last visited the Northern Territory, Begram's soldiers were there.

They've been sieging the region, controlling every activity-trade, passage, even the villages' daily lives. The land's importance is no secret, and Begram is trying to gain complete dominion over it."

Arian's brow furrowed. "And Father-Darius?"

The commander hesitated but finally continued.

"King Darius tried to resolve the situation diplomatically. He wanted Begram's forces to withdraw, arguing that the Northern Territory should remain open for all kingdoms. But during the discussions, one of Begram's troops defied him. He drew his sword against Darius, and for that... Darius retaliated."

"How?" Arian's voice was sharp.

Commander Ashwavarna lowered his gaze. "With his own sword, my lord. He thrust it into the soldier's throat, piercing through his skull. It was... a message.
A warning to Begram not to interfere with our trade and business."

Arian's fists clenched at his sides. "And the villagers?
Why did they vanish?"

Ashwavarna sighed deeply. "The villagers escaped out of fear. They had seen what Begram's armies were doing and what our king did in response.

Caught between two powers, they fled — perhaps believing it was the only way to survive."

The silence that followed was heavy, broken only when Aryanath cleared his throat.
"There's more, Arian."
Arian turned toward him, his eyes narrowing.

"More?"
Aryanath stood, unrolling another parchment to reveal the same strange symbol. "This symbol... we've deciphered it. It's connected to Begram. Their markings are on it, and it isn't just a warning—it's a claim. A declaration that if Kandahar interferes with their troops on the Northern Territory, the consequences will be severe."

Arian's voice dropped to a whisper. "Why? Why are they so concerned with this land?"

Aryanath's face darkened. "Because of the hidden edicts."

"What edicts?"

"The ancient ones-written by our ancestors," Aryanath explained gravely. "They knew the importance of the Northern Territory long before we did. Those edicts are a map, written in coded form, to reveal strategically significant locations in the region."
Arian frowned, confused. "Locations? Why would they care about that?"

"Because those locations are not just ordinary land," Aryanath replied, his voice low. "The edicts speak of treasures buried beneath the soil. Our ancestors called it liquid gold. In the times to come, it will be the greatest treasure of all treasures-more valuable than gold, jewels, or silk. That's why Kandahar holds these secrets so close, and that's why Begram is trying to seize control of the Northern Territory."

Arian took a step back, stunned. "Liquid gold...."
Aryanath nodded. "The heart of trade and power.
Whoever controls the Northern Territory controls the future."

Commander Ashwavarna added solemnly, "Begram understands this now. And so does Our King Darius."
Arian's head swam. He turned back to Aryanath.
"You still haven't told me how Begram learned about the hidden edicts."

Aryanath looked away, his reluctance clear.

"What aren't you telling me?" Arian pressed, his voice growing tense.

Aryanath sighed heavily, finally meeting Arian's gaze.
"It was your father, Arian."

Arian froze. "What?"

"He knew of the edicts-he was Rajvanta's son, after all. He told Zarif, a man who turned traitor. Zarif took that knowledge and betrayed us to Begram.

When Darius learned of your father's actions, he spared him... as he was the son of our warrior turned martyr, but banished him from Kandahar forever."
Arian's voice trembled with anger and disbelief. "My father... betrayed us?"

Aryanath's expression softened. "He thought he was doing what was right. He trusted the wrong man, and Kandahar paid the price."

Arian's chest tightened. Whom do I trust? The question echoed in his mind. His father. Darius.
Kandahar. Begram. Each side wore masks of truth, yet their stories tore at him. Both sides had his own people!
"And why now?" Arian whispered, his voice raw.

"Why are the edicts surfacing now?"

Aryanath's voice carried an ominous weight. "Because the Northern Territory is losing its grip over its own people, Arian. The Kingdom of Begram knows this. Now is the right time to take control of the area. And if Kandahar doesn't defend its legacy, another kingdom will."
Arian turned away, his thoughts a storm of rage and confusion. His father's betrayal. Darius' ruthlessness.
Begram's threats. And at the centre of it all, a land bleeding from greed and power.

He clenched his jaw. "I'll find the truth. I'll visit Begram with Vajra. Menander has answers, and I intend to get them."

Aryanath nodded, though his expression was troubled. "Be careful, Arian. The closer you get to the truth, the sharper the knives become."

Arian's gaze burned with resolve as he left the hall. If the past held ties that bound him, he would tear them free. The truth would not escape him, no matter how deep it was buried.

Chapter 14 - The Unbreakable Bond

The early morning light filtered through the stained-glass windows of the palace, casting soft hues of gold and saffron across the stone floors. Arian stood in the corridor outside Kyra's chambers, staring at the wooden door as if summoning the courage to enter.

His journey to Begram loomed ahead, but before he departed, he needed to see her-his mother, his anchor, the woman who had raised him with unwavering love and tenderness.

As he stepped into the room, a familiar warmth greeted him. Kyra was seated near the window, her face illuminated by the sunlight. Though still recovering from the brutal attack, her posture was regal, her strength evident even in her frailty.

"Mother," Arian said softly, the word carrying a weight of gratitude he could never fully express.

Kyra looked up, a smile breaking through her exhaustion. "Arian, my son. Come closer."
He crossed the room and knelt beside her, his larger hand enveloping hers. "How are you feeling?"

"I've faced worse," she said with a faint chuckle, though her voice was tinged with weariness. "You know I'm not one to be brought down easily."

Arian smiled faintly but said nothing, his thoughts drifting to the memories of his childhood—a time when Kyra had been his entire world. He remembered a moment as vividly as if it had happened yesterday.
He had been six years old, a reckless boy eager to prove himself. The palace grounds had been his playground, and on that fateful day, he had insisted on riding one of the younger, untamed horses.

Despite the stable master's warnings, Arian had mounted the animal, his tiny hands clutching the reins.

The horse had bucked violently, and before he could regain control, he was thrown to the ground. The sharp pain of his broken arm and the fear of the moment had left him sobbing uncontrollably.

Kyra had come running, her face pale with worry.
She had scooped him into her arms as if he weighed nothing, cradling him against her chest. "My sweet boy," she had whispered, her voice trembling. "You're going to be fine. I'm here. I'll always be here."
She had stayed by his side day and night, tending to him with a devotion that defied explanation. Arian had been too young to understand the depth of her love, but now, as a grown man, he saw it clearly. She had been his shield, his sanctuary.

"You're thinking about something," Kyra said, her voice drawing him back to the present.

Arian looked at her, his eyes soft. "I was thinking about the time I fell from the horse."

Kyra's lips curved into a knowing smile. "You scared me half to death that day. But even then, you were fearless. Stubborn as ever."

"You were the one who kept me strong," Arian admitted. "You've always been the reason I could face anything."

Kyra's expression softened, her hand reaching up to cup his cheek. "And you've always been my son. You and Vajra are my greatest blessings."

Arian's chest tightened with emotion. He knew he wasn't Kyra's blood, but she had never treated him as anything less than her own child. He thought of the day Kyra had found him—a two-year-old boy crying in the corner of the palace kitchen.

Kyra had been tending to her daughter, Vajra, when she heard the muffled cries. Following the sound, she had found him—a small, frightened child with tear-streaked cheeks and wide, searching eyes. When she asked the palace staff about him, she learned that his parents had abandoned him, fleeing the kingdom under the weight of their own misdeeds.

Kyra hadn't hesitated. She had taken the boy in, raising him as her own alongside Vajra. She had loved him with the same intensity, never allowing anyone to make him feel like he didn't belong. In her eyes, destiny had

given her two children, and she would protect
them with her life.

"Mother," Arian began, his voice thick with
emotion.
"I owe you everything. I don't know what my
life would've been without you."

Kyra's smile was bittersweet. "You owe me
nothing, my son. You've given me more joy
than I could ever ask for. Watching you and
Vajra grow into the people you are today has
been my greatest pride."

At that moment, Vajra entered the room, her
presence commanding as always. She walked
to Kyra's side and knelt beside her brother.
"Mother, are you feeling better?"

Kyra nodded, brushing a stray strand of hair
from Vajra's face. "I am. But I'm more
concerned about the two of you."

Arian and Vajra exchanged a glance.

Kyra's expression turned serious. "Listen to
me, both of you. This journey to Begram...
it's dangerous. The man who attacked me
was one of their soldiers, disguised as one of
our own. He managed to infiltrate our
troops, and your father dealt with him swiftly.

But this shows how far Begram is willing to
go."
"We'll be cautious," Vajra assured her. "We
know what's at stake."

Kyra shook her head. "It's not enough to be
cautious.
You need to be vigilant. The last time Vajra
went to Begram, they knew it was a
diplomatic visit. But now they're aware that
we know their motives. They'll see this as a
threat, and they'll try to undermine you."

Arian placed a reassuring hand on her
shoulder.
"We'll be ready, Mother. We won't let them
catch us off guard."

Kyra's eyes glistened with unshed tears.
"Promise me you'll take care of each other.
You're my heart, both of you. I couldn't bear
it if anything happened to you."

"We promise," Vajra said, her voice steady.

Kyra pulled them both into an embrace,
holding them tightly. For a moment, the
room was silent, filled only with the
unspoken bond they shared—a love forged

through years of sacrifice and unwavering
devotion.

As Arian and Vajra rose to leave, Kyra called
out one last time. "Arian, Vajra... trust each
other, above all else. And trust yourselves.
No matter what lies ahead, remember that
you carry the strength of Kandahar in your
hearts."

With those words echoing in their minds,
they departed, their path leading them toward
Begram and the truths that awaited them
there.

Chapter 15 - Den of Surprises

Vajra and Arian entered the grand courtroom of Begram, their steps steady but minds vigilant. The room was expansive, with high vaulted ceilings painted with intricate murals of Begram's victories and golden chandeliers that bathed everything in a regal glow. The courtiers whispered amongst themselves as the two Kandahari diplomats made their way to the centre. The tension in the air was palpable, a mix of curiosity, suspicion, and veiled hostility.

At the far end of the courtroom sat Menander, the Prince of Begram, flanked by his advisors. Beside him were two unfamiliar faces. One was a lean, sharp-eyed man dressed in elaborate robes with the insignia of a military strategist on his chest. The other was a woman with a striking presence, her piercing gaze cutting through the room like a blade.

Her dark hair was tied back, and her posture radiated authority. The courtiers around them whispered names - General Tarek and Lady Sirona, key figures in Begram's court and rumoured to be the masterminds behind its growing influence.

Vajra stepped forward, her voice calm yet commanding. "Honourable Prince Menander, members of Begram's esteemed court, we stand here as representatives of Kandahar, not as adversaries but as diplomats seeking resolution. Both our kingdoms are aware of the animosity that has festered between us over the years, fuelled by political and strategic disputes. It is time to address these issues with clarity and fairness."

The courtiers leaned in, their murmurs dying down as Vajra continued. "Kandahar wishes to assure Begram that we have no intentions of intruding upon your sovereignty. However, we do have one pressing request - Begram must cease interfering with our trade routes and recognize the Northern Territory as a shared region."

At the mention of the Northern Territory, a ripple of unrest spread through the courtroom. Courtiers exchanged uneasy glances, and a low murmur of discontent arose. Even Menander stiffened in his seat, his fingers tightening on the armrest of his gilded throne.

"The Northern Territory belongs to no single kingdom," Vajra pressed on, undeterred by the commotion. "It has historically served as a neutral ground for trade and commerce. Any attempt to monopolise it is a direct threat to peace. Kandahar will not tolerate such claims."

Menander's lips curled into a measured smile, though his eyes betrayed a flicker of annoyance. He raised a hand, silencing the whispers. "As our esteemed guest has suggested," he began, his voice smooth but layered with ambiguity, "Begram has no desire to disrupt trade. However, let us not forget that the people of the Northern Territory are of Begram's origin. Their customs, their beliefs-they align with ours. It is only natural that Begram ensures their welfare, and in doing so, the region remains under our protection."

Before Vajra could respond, Arian stepped forward, his tone sharp and unyielding. "The people of the Northern Territory do not belong to any kingdom. As our records state, they lived as an independent unit, governing themselves without the oversight of either Begram or Kandahar. To claim otherwise is to rewrite history."

The tension in the room escalated. Menander leaned slightly toward General Tarek and Lady Sirona, whispering in low tones. The courtiers watched, their expressions a mixture of intrigue and unease. After a moment, Menander straightened and announced,
"The matter is of great significance and warrants deeper discussion. We will reconvene tomorrow to continue this dialogue. For now, let us set aside our differences and enjoy an evening of Begram's hospitality. A gala awaits you in the royal gardens."

With that, Menander rose, the courtiers bowing as he exited the room with his advisors.

That evening, Arian and Vajra arrived at the royal garden, and they couldn't help but marvel at its splendour. The garden was transformed into a vision of opulence, with pathways lined with glowing candles and arches adorned with cascading flowers in hues of crimson, gold, and ivory. Golden vases filled with exotic blooms stood at intervals, their fragrance mingling with the crisp evening air.

Silver trays laden with delicacies floated through the crowd, carried by attendants dressed in Begram's traditional attire. Musicians played soft, hypnotic tunes, their instruments weaving a melody that felt almost otherworldly.

At the centre of the garden, masked dancers performed a mesmerising belly dance, their movements fluid and hypnotic. Their veils shimmered in the candlelight, adding an air of mystery to their performance. Vajra watched the spectacle with admiration but kept her guard up, her sharp eyes scanning the crowd for any signs of duplicity.

Arian, too, was entranced by the beauty of the setting, but his instincts told him to remain cautious.

As he sipped from a silver goblet, a masked woman approached him, her movements deliberate yet graceful. She leaned close and

whispered, "Come with me. There's
something you need to see."

Arian glanced at Vajra, who gave him a
warning look.
"Be careful," she said, her tone firm.

The masked woman led Arian through a
labyrinth of corridors until they reached a
small wooden chamber tucked away from the
festivities. The air was thick with the scent of
aged wood and parchment. She turned to
face him, slowly removing her veil.

"Lira," Arian said flatly, his expression
unreadable.
Lira met his gaze, her confidence
unwavering. "You don't seem surprised to see
me."
Arian didn't respond back
Lira's eyes narrowed, but she pressed on,
producing a scroll from the folds of her robe.
"Your birth mother wanted you to have this,"
she said, handing it to him. "It belongs to
you."

Arian hesitated before taking the scroll,
unrolling it to reveal an intricate map with
ancient symbols.

"Royal blood runs in your veins, Arian," Lira
said, her voice taking on a persuasive tone.
"Your parents lived like outcasts, sacrificing
everything so you could rise to your rightful
place. This edict holds the key to your
destiny. The symbols mark locations where
liquid gold lies buried-wealth and power
beyond imagination."

Arian's grip tightened on the scroll, his mind
racing.
"You know the truth," Lira continued. "Darius
will never let you take his place. Kandahar
will always see you as a shadow of your
ancestors. But Begram can help you.
Together, we can seize the Northern
Territory, and you-Arian, son of a royal
lineage-can claim the throne. No more living
in the shadow of another's crown."

Her words were laced with temptation, each
syllable crafted to sow doubt and ambition.
Arian's face remained stoic, but inside, his
thoughts churned.
"Blood is thicker than water," Lira pressed.
"Your family has fought for this moment.
They knew you were safer in the palace as a
child, but now it's time to take your destiny
into your own hands. With Begram's
support, you can forge your path and ensure
your name is remembered for generations."

Arian stared at the scroll, the weight of her words sinking in. The symbols seemed to pulse with a hidden power, and for a moment, the room felt suffocating. His thoughts spiralled as he stood on the precipice of a decision that could alter the course of his life-and his kingdom-forever.

Chapter 16 - The Evil's Eye

Arian returned to Vajra in the royal guest quarters, his face carefully neutral, concealing the whirlwind of emotions beneath. He had spent the last hour replaying Lira's words, trying to make sense of her sudden appearance and the cryptic edict she had handed him.
Vajra noticed his hesitation and raised an eyebrow.

"Where have you been?"

Arian shrugged casually. "Nowhere significant," he said, leaning back in his chair. "Just a girl being... curious about me." He chuckled softly, masking his unease.
Vajra smirked, sensing an opportunity to tease him.

"Oh, really? 'Curious,' you say? I didn't know you were such a charmer, brother."

"Careful, Vajra," Arian retorted with mock
seriousness, "I might outshine your royal
diplomacy with my sheer magnetism."
Vajra shook her head, a faint smile breaking
across her lips as she watched him banter.
"You are impossible,"
 she said with a mix of fondness and
exasperation.
Vajra, however, wasn't ready to let him off so
easily.

"Come on, Arian. Don't be shy. Who is this
'curious' admirer?"

Arian leaned forward, his voice dropping into
a conspiratorial tone. "Let's just say... she was
very interested in my politics. And, well
"He paused dramatically, feigning a wistful
sigh. "I guess I have a way with the ladies."

Vajra burst into laughter, shaking her head.
"Oh, spare us the details, 'King of Hearts.
We've got bigger things to focus on than your
love life."

Vajra watched him with a mixture of
amusement and concern, her sharp eyes
catching the flicker of something deeper in
Arian's expression. She decided to let it go,
for now, choosing to enjoy the rare moment
of levity between them.

Later that night, in the heart of Begram's opulent palace, Lira entered Menander's chambers. The glow of golden lanterns cast intricate shadows on the walls, and hall was filled with the scent of spiced wine and incense.
Menander was seated by the window, gazing out at the city lights below, but turned sharply when he heard her approach. A slow, satisfied smile spread across his face as he took in her presence.

"Well?" he asked, his voice smooth and expectant.

"It's done," Lira said simply, her tone laced with pride.
Menander rose, his expression triumphant. "My clever, cunning Lira," he murmured, stepping closer.

He placed his hands gently on her waist, his touch both possessive and admiring. "You've done more than I could have hoped for. Arian's parents were sold for mere coin, but their son—" he laughed softly, almost cruelly- "their son has been sold for a kingdom and a dream."

He tilted her chin upward, his dark eyes gleaming with pride and mischief. "You honey-trapped him perfectly. The bond between Kandahar's leaders is broken. Their unity is splintered. They'll never trust each other again."

Lira smiled faintly, her eyes gleaming with satisfaction.

"It wasn't difficult. Arian is vulnerable, torn between loyalty and ambition. He's a pawn who doesn't even realise he's on the board." Menander chuckled, his voice thick with pride. "My brilliant Lira, you're unmatched. You've done what no army could achieve. Kandahar is already in pieces, and soon, it will be nothing but a relic of the past. From this day forward, Begram will reign supreme. The Northern Territory, Kandahar, and every trade route will bow to us. We will be unstoppable."

He stepped closer, brushing a strand of hair from her face. "You've given me victory, my dear. And for that, I owe you everything."

Menander pulled her into a tight embrace, his touch lingering with an air of possessive gratitude. Lira leaned into him briefly, her mind already spinning with thoughts of the battle ahead.

"We must prepare," Menander said, his voice dark with determination. "The time has come to claim what is rightfully ours." Saying this Menander kissed Lira passionately and laid her beneath him on the bed.

As the night deepened, the palace corridors remained silent, but the air was charged with tension. The first move in Begram's deadly game had been played, and the stakes were higher than ever.

Chapter 17 - Torchbearer of Kandahar

The court at Begram had been tense, a place where every word carried the weight of kingdoms. Yet, somehow, Arian had managed to guide the negotiations to Kandahar's favour. The political storm had cleared, but as their chariot rumbled through the narrow mountain passes back toward Kandahar, Arian felt an undercurrent of uncertainty that only Vajra's presence helped to steady.

The chariot was laden with the gifts Menander had sent as tokens of goodwill-silks, jewels, and even rare spices. Yet, the most precious cargo they carried was the delicate treaty they had forged: a truce that promised peace for the Northern Territory and prosperity for both realms.

Vajra broke the silence first, her gaze fixed on the horizon. "Menander is a capable leader," she mused.
"He may refuse the title of king, but in every way that matters, he's already ruling Begram. It's impressive, given his father's condition."

Arian glanced sideways at her. "He's pragmatic.
That's why this worked."

Vajra turned to him with a curious gleam in her eye.
"Speaking of 'this' —what exactly did you say to them in the courtroom? How did you convince Menander and his council to agree to terms so favourable for us?"

Arian smirked, leaning back and resting his arms behind his head. "You still doubt my capabilities? You don't know how persuasive your brother can be."

Vajra laughed, a genuine, melodic sound that softened the tension lingering between them. "Oh, I'm well aware of your silver tongue. But this... this was different. You didn't just charm them, did you?"

Arian's grin widened, but his tone grew more serious.

"Menander understands the value of stability. Begram's resources are stretched thin. They can't afford another conflict, especially not one with us. I made them see that trade and mutual respect were the only logical paths forward."

Vajra nodded, her expression thoughtful. "So, we did it then. The Northern Territory is free from Begram's interference. It's a free dominion now, and that benefits us all."

"It does," Arian agreed. "No more political meddling.

Trade routes remain open. Begram and Kandahar stand as equals, not adversaries. For once, pragmatism triumphed over arrogance."

Vajra's gaze softened as she looked at him. "It's surprising, but this alliance... it's what we needed.

Begram and Kandahar working together-peace and progress. It's almost too good to be true."

~

The sun was setting as their chariot rolled into the gates of Kandahar. The city's golden spires gleamed in the fading light, a beacon of their homecoming.

After unloading the gifts and exchanging quick greetings with the palace guards, Arian and Vajra headed straight to Kyra's chambers.

Inside, Darius was already seated, reviewing a scroll with his usual air of focus and authority. As they entered, he looked up, his face revealing little.
"How was your diplomatic conversation with Begram?" he asked, his voice calm but weighted.

Vajra answered with a confident smile. "It went smoothly, Father. This time, Arian handled the matter very well. He convinced them to agree to our terms."

Darius's expression remained unreadable, his gaze lingering on Arian. The silence that followed was heavy, almost scrutinising.

Kyra, sitting near the window, spoke up, her voice warm with pride. "I told you, Darius," she said, her eyes sparkling as she looked at Arian. "One day, he would make you proud."

Darius didn't respond immediately. Instead, he rose and gestured for Arian to follow him. "Come with me," he said simply, his tone brooking no argument.

In Darius's Counsel Chamber

The chamber was dim, lit only by a few flickering oil lamps. The air was thick with the unspoken history between the two men. Arian stood in the centre, arms crossed, his face carefully composed. Across from him, Darius leaned against the large oak desk, his expression just as guarded.
For years, their relationship had been strained— defined more by duty than affection. Arian respected Darius as the King of Kandahar but had never truly accepted him as a father. There had always been a distance between them, an invisible wall built from years of misunderstandings, resentment, and silence.
Darius was the embodiment of authority, a figure who inspired both awe and fear. But for Arian, the fatherly warmth he had longed for was absent. The man before him was a king—a ruler first, a father second.

Breaking the silence, Darius spoke, his voice low and measured.

"Arian, I know you've struggled to accept me as your father. And I don't blame you."

Arian's jaw tightened, but he said nothing.

"I made decisions," Darius continued, "that shaped your life in ways you didn't choose. I was the one who ordered your parents to leave. I did it as a king, not as a father. And for that, I know you've hated me."
Arian's expressions were cold.

Darius didn't flinch. "You deserve the truth." He paused, his gaze steady. "Your parents... they weren't what they seemed. Their ambitions were dangerous
—for you, for Kandahar, for everything we stand for.
Leaving you here wasn't just an act of protection; it was a necessity for them. I knew that this day would come. And I will never come in your path. Whatever you choose is fine. Because you have all the rights to choose your own path."

Arian's breath hitched, but he quickly masked it.

"I know I failed you," Darius said, his voice softening.

"I may not have been the father you wanted, but you have always been my son in my heart. And Kyra... she has always loved you unconditionally. Through her, I learned what it means to love without expectation or fear. To love without limits. She is the torchbearer, the light we all seek in our lives. I am not as expressive as her, but I love you my dear son."

Arian's composure began to waver. He clenched his fists, trying to hold onto the emotion that hadn't been surfaced for so long.

"I was always afraid," Darius admitted, "that your
parents would return one day to tear you away from us. That fear made me distant. But it never stopped me from caring for you. If you've ever felt unloved, know that it wasn't because of you. It was because I was a coward. I feared before I loved."
Tears welled in Darius's eyes as he continued, his voice breaking. "If you choose to side with Begram, I won't stop you. You are free to make your own decisions. But if we meet on the battlefield..." He faltered, swallowing hard. "Kill me, Arian. Strike me down, because I will never raise my sword

against you. I can fight the whole world, but I cannot fight my own son."

The weight of his words hung heavy in the air. For the first time, Darius's walls crumbled, revealing the raw, unfiltered love he had kept buried for years.

"All that I have is yours," Darius said, his voice barely above a whisper. "My heart belongs to you."

Arian's stoic facade shattered. A deep, shuddering breath escaped him, and he stepped forward, his emotions overwhelming him. Tears streamed down his face as he gripped Darius's arms, his voice breaking. "I'm sorry," Arian choked out, his body trembling. "I didn't know... I didn't understand."

Darius pulled him into an embrace, holding him tightly as Arian sobbed against his chest. Years of pain, anger, and longing poured out in a flood of tears.

"I've always been proud of you," Darius whispered, his own tears falling. "And I always will be."
In that moment, the distance between them dissolved, replaced by a bond that was raw,

fragile, and deeply human. Father and son stood together, united not by blood, but by the love that had endured in silence for too long.

Chapter 18 - The Battle of the Old City

The war council convened in Kandahar's grand hall, a room charged with urgency and solemn determination. Darius, Aryanath, Kyra, Vajra, Arian, and Commander Ashwavarna sat around an ornately carved wooden table illuminated by flickering torches. On the table lay a detailed map of the Northern Territory, its rivers, mountain ranges, and key trade routes marked in vivid ink. This was not just a battle over land—it was a battle for Kandahar's identity, sovereignty, and the legacy of its people.

Arian unrolled the ancient edict he had received from Lira, his face stoic but his mind racing. The faded parchment bore the royal seal of Kandahar, a stark reminder of what had been stolen from them years ago. He handed it to Kyra and Aryanath, whose scholarly eyes immediately recognised its significance.

Kyra's voice broke the tense silence. "This edict... it's ours. It's the missing piece that Zarif took when he betrayed us. For years, Begram has used it to lay claim to territories that were rightfully ours, territories built by the blood and sweat of our ancestors."

Aryanath nodded, his tone somber. "This document is proof of Kandahar's rightful ownership. Without it, Begram's claim crumbles. If we let them hold onto it, they'll use it as leverage to expand their control. We cannot allow that."

Darius's gaze darkened as he studied the map. His voice, low and steady, carried the weight of his years as a warrior and king. "This battle is not just about reclaiming a piece of paper. It's about defending the sacrifices of our ancestors. The Battle of Arachosia was fought for the western frontier, a land that was barren when we claimed it but now thrives because of our people's labor. Rajvanta, our great warrior, your grandfather, fought with courage and valour to secure that victory. He bled for this kingdom so that we could prosper."

Darius's voice grew more fervent, his words carrying a fire that sparked in the hearts of everyone present.

"We owe it to them-the warriors who gave their lives, the families who endured loss, the people who built this kingdom brick by brick-not to let their sacrifices be in vain. If we lose now, we lose more than land. We lose our history, our pride, and our future. This time, we fight for the Northern Territory.

And this time, we will make it ours before the enemy sets foot on it."

Arian listened intently, the guilt of his earlier doubts mixing with newfound resolve. He raised his head, meeting Darius's gaze. "They think I'll fight for Begram. They believe I'm their pawn. Let them. I'll use their arrogance against them. I'll lead them into a trap they won't see coming."

Commander Ashwavarna leaned forward, his deep voice cutting through the room. "Arian's insight into their plans gives us an edge. But we need more than brute force to win this battle. Begram's forces outnumber us. They have siege engines, cavalry, and fortified positions. If we meet them head-on, we risk losing everything."

Aryanath interjected, his scholarly demeanour giving way to sharp strategy. "We need to fight smart, not hard. This is where Guerrilla warfare comes in."

The Guerrilla Warfare Plan :

Guerrilla warfare, Aryanath explained, was the art of unconventional combat-attacking from the shadows, striking swiftly, and retreating before the enemy could react. It relied on agility, deception, and intimate knowledge of the terrain.

"We will use Kandahar's rugged landscape to our advantage," Aryanath continued, tracing the mountain ranges and dense forests on the map. "Our troops will remain hidden, moving through the forests and mountain passes. We'll divide into small, agile units capable of quick attacks. The enemy will never see us coming."

Commander Ashwavarna added, "Our scouts will set ambushes at key chokepoints along their supply routes. Without food, weapons, and reinforcements, Begram's forces will weaken. We'll harass them at night, attacking their camps and cutting off their communications. Fear and exhaustion will become our allies."

Vajra leaned over the map, her eyes blazing with determination. "And when they're disoriented, we strike their command centre. We cut off the head of the snake."

Darius stood, his towering figure exuding authority.
"We'll use decoys to lure their main forces into the valleys, where our archers will have the high ground.
Our siege engines will remain hidden until the enemy exposes their flanks. When they think they have us cornered, we'll unleash everything we have
—catapults, fire arrows, and battering rams. We will turn their arrogance into their downfall."

Arian's voice was steady but laced with emotion. "I'll play my part. I'll feed them just enough information to keep their confidence high. When the moment comes, I'll guide them straight into our trap."

Kyra, who had been silent until now, spoke with quiet strength. "I will guard the palace and its secrets. Aryanath and I will ensure the city remains secure from within. Kandahar will not fall, not from infiltration or treachery."

Before departing, Darius addressed the assembled troops in the palace courtyard. Hundreds of warriors stood in formation, their faces a mixture of resolve and anticipation.

Darius's voice carried across the courtyard, each word striking like a drumbeat.
"Warriors of Kandahar, today we stand on the edge of history.
Behind us lies the legacy of our ancestors, built with their sweat, blood, and sacrifice. Ahead of us lies a battle that will define our future.
 The Northern Territory is not just land—it is our land, cultivated by our people, defended by our soldiers, and sanctified by the sacrifices of those who came before us."

He paused, his gaze sweeping over the crowd. "We will not let the sacrifices of our forefathers go in vain. We will not let the enemies of Kandahar desecrate what is ours. This time, we fight not just for survival but for honour. For pride. For everything we hold dear."

The warriors roared in unison, their swords
raised high.
Darius continued, his voice unwavering.
"When the enemy looks upon us, let them
see the strength of Kandahar. Let them feel
the weight of our courage, our unity, and our
unbreakable resolve. We fight for our
kingdom, for our families, and for the future
of our children. Let us ride into battle with
fire in our hearts and victory in our sights.
For Kandahar!"

The courtyard erupted in a deafening cry of
"For Kandahar!"

March to Battle:

The sun rose over the mountains as Darius,
Arian, Vajra, and Commander Ashwavarna
led the troops out of Kandahar. The army
was a formidable sight— soldiers clad in
gleaming armour, carrying spears, swords,
and shields. Siege engines rumbled behind
them, pulled by oxen. Archers rode
horseback, their quivers filled with arrows
ready to rain death upon the enemy.

In the palace, Kyra watched from the highest
tower, her heart heavy but her resolve
unshaken. Aryanath coordinated with the

city's guards, fortifying the walls and setting traps for any infiltrators.

As the army disappeared into the horizon, the battle for the Northern Territory-and the very soul of Kandahar—had begun.

Chapter 19 - Rise of the New World

The dawn of battle brought a heavy stillness over the Northern Territory. Kandahar's forces, hidden in the dense forests and rugged hills, watched their prey from the shadows. They moved with the precision of wolves, their silence louder than the enemy's clanking armour. This wasn't just war—it was a battle for identity, for survival, for the blood-soaked soil their ancestors had died to protect.

The Art of the Shadows:

Guerrilla warfare was more than a strategy; it was a philosophy of survival and victory through unconventional means. Kandahar's soldiers knew the terrain intimately, every ridge and valley mapped in their minds. They used the land as their weapon, turning it into a fortress of ambushes and traps.

Vajra led one of the key missions, her mind sharp with focus. She had split her forces into smaller units, each assigned a crucial task. The archers hid in high vantage points, their quivers full of arrows dipped in oil to set the enemy ablaze. Infantry units buried caltrops along enemy pathways, while scouts laid silent traps in the dense underbrush.

"It's not just about winning," Vajra whispered to her captains as they reviewed the plan. "It's about making them afraid-breaking their will to fight before they even draw their swords."

Vajra's Siege: The Fire of the North

The night was still as Kandahar's archers unleashed their first volley of flaming arrows. The sky lit up in streaks of orange and gold as the arrows arced through the air, striking the enemy's watchtowers and supply wagons. The wood cracked and splintered as flames consumed the structures, and the camp erupted into chaos.

"Sound the alarm!" shouted a Begramite officer, but his voice was drowned out by the crackling fire and the panicked screams of his soldiers.

Vajra waited until the enemy forces were fully distracted before signalling her infantry. "Go!" she ordered, and her soldiers surged forward like a tidal wave.

The southern gate, reinforced with iron and manned by a dozen soldiers, stood no chance. Using battering rams and sheer determination, Kandahar's infantry broke through. Vajra herself led the charge, her twin blades gleaming in the firelight.

The enemy fought fiercely, but their cohesion crumbled under the relentless assault. Vajra's troops moved like a storm-swift, unpredictable, and devastating. She fought alongside them, her movements precise and deadly. She was not just a leader but a force of nature, cutting through enemy lines with a mix of grace and fury.

At one point, she faced a Begramite captain—a giant of a man wielding a massive battle axe. He swung at her with all his might, the axe whistling through the air. But Vajra was faster. She ducked, her blades flashing as she slashed at his legs. The captain roared in pain, falling to his knees. With a final, decisive strike, Vajra ended him.

Her troops cheered as they pushed deeper into the stronghold. Flames lit up the night, and the Begramite soldiers, disoriented and terrified, began to flee.

Arian's Deception: The Mind of the Fox

In the nearby town, Arian played his role to perfection. Disguised as a defector, he had sown seeds of doubt and confusion within the enemy camp. Zarvon,

 Menander's shrewd advisor, remained skeptical.

"Why would a son of Kandahar betray his people?"

 Zarvon asked, his piercing gaze fixed on Arian.

"Because Kandahar has no place for me," Arian replied, his voice steady and cold. "And because I know your weakness."

Zarvon leaned in, intrigued but cautious. "And what might that be?"

Arian smirked. "Your distrust in your own people."

He handed over a false map detailing Kandahar's supposed troop movements. The enemy swallowed the bait, redirecting their forces to a valley rigged with traps. As the Begramite troops marched, they fell victim to caltrops, ambushes, and hidden archers. The valley became a slaughterhouse, and Arian's deception ensured the enemy's defeat before they could even engage in open combat.

Darius and Ashwavarna: The Heart of the Battlefield

Farther south, Darius and Commander Ashwavarna led a daring strike on the enemy's headquarters. The battlefield was a cacophony of screams, clashing steel, and the thunder of hooves. Smoke from burning siege engines filled the air, stinging the eyes and choking the lungs.

Darius, clad in armour that gleamed in the dim light, fought with the strength of a man who had everything to lose. His sword moved

with precision, cutting down enemies who
dared stand in his way.

His presence on the battlefield was magnetic,
rallying his troops even in the face of
overwhelming odds.

"Remember the sacrifices of our ancestors!"
Darius roared, his voice carrying over the
chaos. "We fight for them, for our land, for
our people! Hold your ground!"
Commander Ashwavarna, leading the
cavalry, executed a textbook flanking
manoeuver. His horsemen swept through the
enemy ranks like a scythe, their lances and
swords cutting down Begramite soldiers with
ruthless efficiency.

Together, Darius and Ashwavarna
dismantled the enemy's command structure,
targeting officers and supply lines. The
Begramite forces, leaderless and
demoralised, began to crumble.

As the chaos of the battlefield raged on,
Arian broke through the enemy lines, his
sword cutting a path toward where Darius
was locked in combat. His instincts drew him
toward the centre of the fray, where his
father, the King of Kandahar, was
surrounded by a ring of Begramite soldiers.

Darius fought with the relentless fury of a
lion defending his pride, his blade moving
with a precision that belied his years. But
even the strongest warriors could not hold
against such overwhelming odds forever.

Arian's chest tightened as he saw an enemy
soldier raise a spear aimed at Darius's
exposed flank
Without hesitation, Arian sprinted forward,
his voice bellowing across the battlefield.

"Father! To your left!"
Darius turned just in time to block the attack,
his sword clanging against the spear's shaft.
Before the soldier could react, Arian was
upon him, delivering a swift and fatal strike to
his chest. Blood splattered across the dusty
ground as the enemy collapsed.

Darius glanced at Arian, his expression
unreadable but his eyes reflecting a flicker of
relief. For a brief moment, they stood side by
side, the chaos of battle swirling around them
like a storm.

"You chose the right side," Darius said gruffly,
his voice barely audible over the clamour.

Arian gave a half-smile, gripping his sword
tighter.

"Let's make sure they regret challenging Kandahar."

Father and Son: A Storm of Fire

Together, they fought like a wildfire spreading uncontrollably, their movements perfectly synchronised as if an unspoken bond had finally emerged between them. Darius, with his years of experience and unyielding strength, moved like an unshakable wall, while Arian, agile and cunning, darted in and out of the enemy ranks like a viper.

When an enemy soldier lunged toward Arian's side, Darius blocked the attack with his shield, countering with a devastating downward slash that split the enemy's sword in two. Arian seized the opening, stepping forward and disarming another opponent with a quick flick of his wrist before delivering a finishing blow.

"Stay close!" Darius barked as the enemy regrouped.
"I should be saying that to you," Arian shot back, parrying an incoming attack.

Despite the chaos, there was a protective energy between them. When Arian found himself momentarily surrounded, Darius surged forward, his sword cutting down the attackers before they could land a single blow.

"Are you hurt?" Darius asked without breaking stride, his voice tight with concern.

"Not a chance," Arian replied, deflecting an arrow that had been aimed at his father's back. "Keep your head in the fight, old man."

A ghost of a smile tugged at Darius's lips. "Old man, is it? Let me show you how an old man fights."

With that, Darius charged forward with renewed vigour, cutting through the enemy ranks like a force of nature. Arian followed closely, their combined might devastating the Begramite forces.

Valour in Chaos

The battlefield seemed to part before them as they fought, the sheer intensity of their partnership driving fear into the hearts of their enemies. Darius's booming voice rallied the Kandahari soldiers nearby.

"Fight for your families! Fight for Kandahar!
Drive them back!"

Arian added his own flair to the moment,
turning to the enemy soldiers and taunting
them. "Run while you can, or face the wrath
of Kandahar's finest!"

His words, combined with their relentless
assault, broke the enemy's resolve. Begramite
soldiers hesitated, their fear palpable.

When an enemy officer charged at Arian, he
leapt into action, intercepting the strike. The
officer was skilled, but Arian's cunning won
out. He feigned a stumble, drawing the
officer closer, and then delivered a brutal
upward slash that sent him crashing to the
ground.

"Nice work," Darius acknowledged, his tone
gruff but genuine.
"Not bad for your son, huh?" Arian quipped,
flashing a grin before they launched into the
next wave of enemies.

As the battle wore on, their protectiveness for
each other became increasingly evident.
When Darius noticed Arian battling multiple
enemies at once, he charged in without a

second thought, his sword cleaving through the attackers.

"You take too many risks," Darius growled, his tone equal parts anger and concern.

"Someone has to keep you on your toes," Arian retorted, but his eyes betrayed his gratitude.

Later, when Darius's leg buckled from a particularly vicious strike, Arian placed himself between his father and the oncoming attackers, deflecting blows with a ferocity that left even Darius momentarily stunned.

"You're not falling here," Arian said firmly, pulling
Darius to his feet.

"Nor are you," Darius replied, steadying himself and standing tall once more.

The Turning Point

Their unrelenting assault and the synergy of their movements became the rallying cry for Kandahar's forces. Soldiers who had been wavering found their courage renewed as they

watched the king and his son fight side by
side.

"Push forward!" Arian shouted, his voice
carrying over the battlefield.

"For Kandahar!" Darius roared, raising his
sword high.
Together, they led the charge that broke the
enemy's final line of defence. Arian's cunning
tactics and Darius's indomitable will proved
an unstoppable combination.

For the first time, Arian saw not just a king
but a father—a man who had fought with
everything he had to protect his son and his
kingdom. And Darius saw not just a warrior
but the son he had always hoped would stand
by his side.

In that fleeting moment of silence, amidst the
wreckage of war, the bond between father
and son finally began to heal.

Chaos in the Enemy Camp

The once-disciplined Begramite army was
now a picture of chaos. Soldiers ran in all
directions, their formations shattered.
Supplies burned, and morale plummeted.

Zarvon, realising too late that Arian had deceived them, tried to regroup the remaining forces.

Menander, standing in the middle of the chaos, refused to retreat. "We hold this ground!" he bellowed, his voice a mix of anger and desperation.

"We are Begram's might! We do not yield!"

But even Menander's courage couldn't turn the tide.
Kandahar's forces were relentless, their guerrilla tactics dismantling Begram's army piece by piece.

Vajra's Triumph

Back at the stronghold, Vajra stood victorious. Her blades were bloodied, her armour dented, but her spirit was unbroken. She climbed to the highest tower, where Kandahar's banner was raised for all to see.

"This is our land," she declared, her voice steady and strong.
"We have taken back what was stolen from us. Let no enemy dare challenge Kandahar again."

Her troops erupted in cheers, their voices echoing across the battlefield.

The final assault on the Kingdom of Begram began under the cover of the crimson sunrise, the light spilling over the battlefield like fire. Kandahar's warriors stood tall, their armour glinting as they gathered their strength for one last push to reclaim the lands that were rightfully theirs. Darius led the charge, flanked by Arian, Commander Ashwavarna, and Vajra, their collective presence a force of unshakable resolve.

The battlefield was a chaotic symphony of clashing swords, war cries, and the thunder of horses' hooves.
Begram's forces had drawn a final line of defence, their soldiers forming a net of steel and shields to protect their leader, Menander, who stood within his command post. But Kandahar's warriors were relentless, their tactics honed and their will unbroken.

Breaking the Shield: Arian and Ashwavarna's Assault

Arian charged ahead into the first line of enemy soldiers, his sword an extension of his fury. With each strike, he cut down the defenders, his movements precise and ruthless. His eyes burned with determination as he carved a path through the enemy ranks. Begramite soldiers fell before him, their formation faltering under his relentless assault.

Behind him, Commander Ashwavarna rallied their forces. "Break their net! Leave them no room to regroup!" he roared, his deep voice cutting through the chaos.

Darius and Ashwavarna worked in perfect unison, their combined strategies devastating the enemy ranks. Ashwavarna's troops attacked from the flanks, splintering the enemy's tight shield wall, while Darius charged into the weakened centre, his massive presence like a battering ram.

"Drive them back!" Darius bellowed, swinging his sword with a force that sent shields and soldiers flying. He moved like a storm, unstoppable and unyielding.

As the enemy's net of defence began to crumble, Arian and Ashwavarna exploited the gaps with tactical precision. Arian's strikes were quick and lethal, dispatching enemy captains before they could rally their troops. The soldiers of Begram began to scatter, their formation breaking under Kandahar's sheer force.

The Cavalry of Vajra: A Leap Toward Victory

Amid the chaos, Vajra, mounted on her trusted warhorse, led the cavalry to the heart of the enemy's defences. Her eyes locked on Menander, the figure at the centre of the enemy's crumbling command.
Determined to end the battle and secure Kandahar's victory, she signalled her troops to spread out and clear the way.

Menander's forces scrambled to shield their leader, forming a desperate last line of defence. Vajra's horse reared, its muscles coiling with energy as it prepared for a leap that would defy expectations.

"Clear the path!" Vajra shouted, her voice sharp and commanding.

Her horse charged forward, picking up speed as it approached the barricade of soldiers. With a mighty leap, the horse launched itself into the air, soaring above the heads of Menander's remaining guards.

Time seemed to slow as Vajra, her sword raised high, balanced perfectly atop her steed.

She descended like an avenging force, her blade gleaming in the sunlight. Menander barely had time to raise his weapon before Vajra's sword plunged into his chest with deadly precision. The force of her strike drove him backward, his lifeblood spilling onto the battlefield. His eyes widened in shock, then dulled as life drained from him.

Vajra dismounted gracefully, her horse landing beside her with a thud. She stood over Menander's fallen body, her blade still buried in his chest. The battlefield seemed to hold its breath as she raised her sword, now slick with the blood of Kandahar's enemy.

"For Kandahar!" she cried, her voice ringing out like a clarion call.

Her troops erupted into cheers, their spirits ignited by her courage and valour. The sight of their leader striking down Menander sent waves of panic through the enemy forces, who began to retreat in disarray.

The Final Push

While Vajra's bold assault struck a decisive blow to the enemy's morale, Darius and Arian seized the moment to press their advantage. The father-son duo fought side by side, their movements a harmonious blend of experience and youthful energy.
Darius's strikes were heavy and devastating, shattering shields and scattering the enemy like dry leaves in a storm. Arian moved like a shadow, quick and deadly, his sword finding every weak point in the enemy's armour
.

Together with Ashwavarna, they pushed forward, shattering what remained of the enemy's resistance.
The Begramite forces, leaderless and demoralised, fled the battlefield, leaving behind weapons and wounded comrades.

The Aftermath:

As the dust settled, Kandahar's soldiers stood victorious. The battlefield was littered with

the remnants of Begram's once-mighty army,
their banners trampled and broken.

Vajra turned to her troops. "This is our
victory," she said, her voice steady despite the
weight of the battle.
"But it is not just mine. It belongs to every
soldier who fought today, to every family we
protect, and to every life we honour."

Darius approached her, his armour battered
but his presence unbowed. "You've done us
proud," he said, placing a hand on her
shoulder.
Arian and Ashwavarna joined them, their
expressions reflecting both exhaustion and
triumph.

The four stood together, a symbol of
Kandahar's resilience and unity.

"Our ancestors would be proud," Darius said,
his voice filled with emotion. "We've
reclaimed what is ours. And we will honour
their sacrifices by protecting it with everything
we have."

Vajra, her sword still in hand, nodded.
"Kandahar stands stronger than ever."

The battle was nearing its conclusion, the enemy forces shattered and scattered. Amidst the chaos, Arian moved swiftly through the shadows of the battlefield, his purpose singular. His blade was already stained with the blood of Begram's soldiers, but his mind was elsewhere-on Lira, the woman who had haunted his thoughts since her betrayal.

He found her in the ruins of an abandoned watchtower at the edge of the battlefield, where she stood, waiting for him. The flickering light of a distant fire danced across her face, illuminating her sharp features and the cold resolve in her eyes. She held a curved dagger in her hand, its blade gleaming ominously.
"So, you came," Lira said, her voice steady, almost serene. "I knew you would."

Arian stopped a few paces away, his sword gripped tightly in his hand. His chest heaved from the effort of battle, but his eyes were fixed on her, unreadable.

"Why?" he asked, his voice low but laced with anger.

"Why betray me, Lira? Why give Begram the means to destroy us?"

Lira's lips curled into a faint, bitter smile. "You still don't see it, do you? This was never about loyalty or betrayal. This was about survival. About power.
Begram offered me what Kandahar never could—a future."

Arian's grip on his sword tightened. "A future built on lies and bloodshed? You call that a future?"

She stepped closer, her dagger raised defensively.

"Don't act like you're above it all, Arian. You've spilled blood just like I have. You've fought for power, for pride, for revenge. We're not so different, you and I."

"No," Arian said firmly, his voice steady. "We are nothing alike. I fight for my people, for my family.

You fight for yourself."

Lira lunged at him suddenly, her dagger aimed for his heart. Arian sidestepped her attack, his reflexes sharp despite his exhaustion. Their blades clashed in a flurry of strikes and parries, each movement calculated and precise.

"You should have stayed out of this war,"
Arian said, his voice strained as he deflected
her attacks. "You should have stayed out of
my life."

Lira laughed, a cold, hollow sound. "And
miss the chance to see the great Arian
brought to his knees?
Never."

Her words fuelled his anger, but Arian kept
his focus.
He waited for the right moment, watching
her movements, predicting her strikes. When
she overextended in her next attack, he
seized the opportunity. With a swift, decisive
motion, he disarmed her, sending her dagger
clattering to the ground.
Lira staggered back, her eyes wide with shock
as Arian levelled his sword at her chest. She
looked at him, a flicker of fear crossing her
face for the first time.
"Do it," she whispered, her voice trembling.
"Finish it."

Arian hesitated for a moment, his grip
tightening on his sword. Memories of their
shared past flashed through his mind-her
laughter, her wit, the moments when he had

trusted her. But those memories were tainted now, overshadowed by her betrayal.

"This is for Kandahar," he said, his voice cold and resolute.

With a swift, powerful thrust, he drove his sword through her chest. Lira gasped, her eyes widening as blood stained her lips. She stumbled, her body collapsing to the ground as Arian withdrew his blade.
For a moment, he stood over her, his chest heaving, his emotions a storm of anger, regret, and finality.
Lira's eyes met his one last time, a mix of defiance and sorrow in their depths.

"You were wrong," Arian said softly, his voice barely audible. "We were never the same."

As the light faded from her eyes, Arian turned away, leaving her lifeless body behind. The echoes of the battlefield called him back, but the weight of her death lingered in his heart. It was a burden he would carry, another scar in the story of his life and the war for Kandahar.

The battlefield echoed with the cheers of their troops as the sun dipped below the horizon, casting a golden glow over the land they had fought so fiercely to defend. Victory was theirs, and with it, the promise of a new era for Kandahar.

Chapter 21 - The Beginning of Eternity

The gates of Kandahar stood wide open, adorned with garlands of flowers, shimmering silks, and golden banners fluttering in the soft breeze. The entire kingdom thrummed with life as people lined the streets, cheering and waving as the returning warriors marched into the city. The clatter of hooves and the rhythmic beat of drums echoed through the air. The sun cast its golden glow over the procession, illuminating the faces of battle-hardened soldiers, their armour still bearing the scars of war but polished to a brilliant shine.

In the royal chariot rode Darius, Vajra, and Arian, their heads held high, their expressions resolute but softened by the joy of victory. Commander Ashwavarna rode beside them, his shoulders squared with

pride, his eyes scanning the crowd, humbled
by the overwhelming cheers. Women threw
flower petals, children clapped with delight,
and elders bowed their heads in respect. The
air was filled with the echoes of celebration,
and for the first time in what felt like an
eternity, hope reigned supreme in Kandahar.

The Grand Ceremony

The royal courtroom of Kandahar had never
looked more magnificent. Its high ceilings
were adorned with golden drapes and
intricate carvings of Kandahar's rich history.
The hall was lit by hundreds of oil lamps and
crystal chandeliers, casting a warm glow over
the gathering. The scent of incense lingered
in the air, mingling with the fragrance of fresh
roses strewn across the floor.

Seated on the high dais were Darius and
Kyra, resplendent in their regal attire. Darius
wore a robe of deep crimson, edged with
gold, while Kyra's gown shimmered like silver
under the light. Their faces glowed with pride
as they looked upon their children and the
warriors who had brought victory to
Kandahar. The crowd erupted in cheers as
Vajra and Arian entered the hall, followed by

Commander Ashwavarna, Aryanath, and the brave soldiers who had fought valiantly on the battlefield.

Kyra stood gracefully and raised her hand to silence the crowd. In her hand, she held a tray of medals and gemstones, each symbolising the gratitude of Kandahar. With a voice filled with emotion, she began, "Today, we honour not just victory but the courage, sacrifice, and unyielding spirit of our people. Each of you has shown what it means to fight for the future of Kandahar, for the legacy of our ancestors, and for the hope of generations to come.
You are the light of this kingdom."

One by one, Kyra presented medals and gemstones to the soldiers, her hands trembling slightly as she pinned a medallion to Vajra's chest and then to Arian's.

When Commander Ashwavarna stepped forward, the hall erupted in cheers once more. Kyra handed him a medallion engraved with the emblem of Kandahar, bowing slightly in respect. "For your strategic brilliance and courage, you will forever be a part of Kandahar's legacy," she said, her voice ringing with sincerity.

Darius Declares the Future

Darius stepped forward, the room falling silent as he raised his hand. His voice was steady and commanding but laced with deep emotion. "Today is not just a day of victory but a day of transformation.

We have defended what is ours, but now it is time to build a future that will stand for eternity. And for this, we need leaders who will guide us with wisdom, courage, and unwavering dedication."
He turned to Vajra, his eyes shining with pride. "The daughter of Kandahar - Vajra, fought with the might of a thousand warriors. Her courage and leadership led us to reclaim the Northern Territory and defend our honour. It is only fitting that she be the one to rule Begram and the Northern Territory. From this day forward, Vajra will be the ruler of these lands, ensuring peace and prosperity for all who dwell there."

The crowd erupted in applause as Vajra stepped forward. She knelt before her father, and Kyra placed a silver crown upon her head. Tears streamed down Kyra's face as she whispered, "You are the light of our family, my brave daughter." Vajra rose, her head held high, the cheers of the crowd echoing through the hall.

Darius then turned to Arian, his voice trembling slightly with emotion. "And now, it is time for Kandahar to have a King who embodies the strength, wisdom, and resilience of our people. My son, Arian, has proven himself worthy. From today onwards, Arian will be the King of Kandahar."

Kyra stepped forward with the golden crown, her hands steady despite the tears in her eyes. She placed it gently on Arian's head, her voice breaking as she said, "Rule with wisdom, my son, and let your heart guide you."

Darius placed his hands on Arian's shoulders, his voice filled with pride. "You are my son, Arian. Today, you are not just my pride but the pride of Kandahar."

Darius continued, "Aryanath, who guarded our kingdom with unwavering resolve, will now be the Chief Advisor of Kandahar. His wisdom will guide us in times of peace and conflict." Aryanath stepped forward, bowing deeply as he received his medallion.

Commander Ashwavarna was honoured once again.

Darius placed a hand on his shoulder. "You have led our troops with brilliance and unmatched valour.
Your name will be etched in the chronicles of Kandahar forever."

Darius addressed the hall once more, his voice rising with enthusiasm and determination. "My people, this victory is not the end; it is the beginning of a new era. We have shown that unity, courage, and sacrifice can overcome any challenge. Let us not rest on our laurels but continue to build a future where our children can thrive.

From today, our Queen and Chief Counsellor Kyra will oversee the geo-strategic affairs of both regions. I will handle international diplomacy. And with our new leaders, King Arian and Ruler Vajra, Kandahar will shine brighter than ever before. Let us pledge to protect our lands, honour our ancestors, and leave behind a legacy of greatness."

The Celebration

As night fell, Kandahar erupted in celebration. The sky was lit with fireworks, their brilliant colours reflecting off the golden spires of the palace. Music filled the air, and

people danced in the streets, their laughter
carrying on the wind.
In the palace courtyard, Arian and Vajra
stood side by side, their crowns gleaming
under the starlit sky.
Kyra and Darius watched from a distance,
their hearts full. Darius turned to Kyra, his
voice soft. "This is the Kandahar I dreamed
of-a kingdom united, a future secure."
Kyra smiled, leaning against him. "And it's
only the beginning."
The night wore on, but the spirit of
Kandahar burned brightly, a beacon of hope
for all who called it home.
The kingdom stood stronger than ever, ready
to embrace its new era-a *beginning of
eternity.*